Survival
Changes
Everything

A Wiley Davis Adventure • Book 2

To all the darling doggies, past and present, in my life! Roo, Eric, Parker, Willow, Murphy, Lucas, Heidi, Sammy, Strider, Brandy, Lucky, Sunny, Luna, and so many others remembered with love.

To the Patrons of my Art, another hearty thank you for the support, love, and many good laughs you continue to supply. If you read my first story, you are part of this much cherished group.

Special thanks to Robert (Bob) Walter who created the cover art and sketches for books I & II. Every piece has surpassed my wildest expectations. I look forward to years of collaboration. To Laura Walter, please keep feeding us your good ideas. Ginger Snider, Julie Wiernik Child, and Val Wiley, thanks for the help of your sharp eyes.

Being able to put the last two manuscripts into the very capable hands of creative director and graphic artist, John Gouin at Graphikitchen added expertise and personal delight to the projects.

Hall and Todd Carlough, thank you both for the phone calls, suggestions, and helping hands as I dream my way through these stories.

I thank Pam Frucci for her encouragement and support to keep moving forward. To those who have, or do live on Grosse Ile, your warm welcome whenever I visit the Island is a pleasure. Throughout this endeavor, I have made many new and enriched several old relationships, making me a very lucky girl!

Lake Superior

Upper Peninsula

Traverse City

Lower Peninsula

UNITED STATES

MICHIGAN

Lake Michigan

Gross

Chicago, IL

Toledo

UNITED STATES

ROUGH SKETCH OF MICHIGAN AND THE GREAT LAKES

Georgian Bay

Lake Huron

CANADA

Lake Ontario

it

Lake St. Clair

Lake Erie

Kelleys Island, OH

N

W   E

S

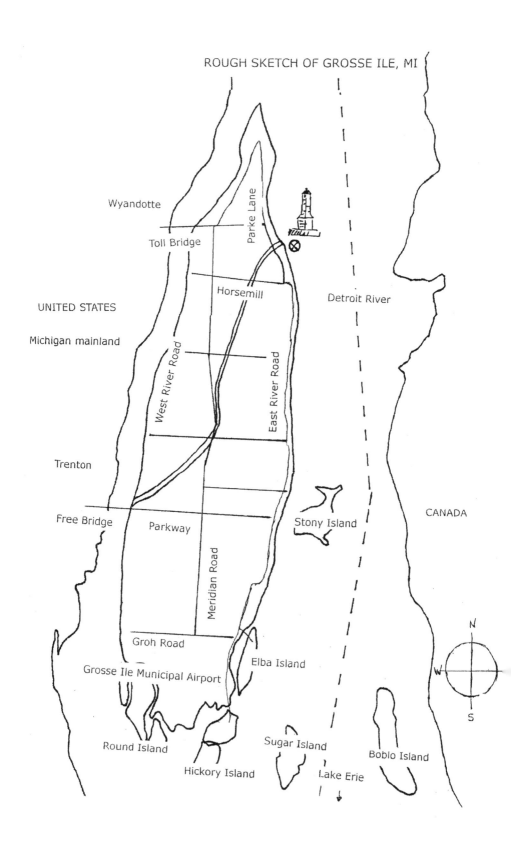

ROUGH SKETCH OF GROSSE ILE, MI

Wyandotte

Toll Bridge

Parke Lane

Horsemill

UNITED STATES

Michigan mainland

West River Road

East River Road

Detroit River

Trenton

Free Bridge

Parkway

Stony Island

CANADA

Meridian Road

Groh Road

Grosse Ile Municipal Airport

Elba Island

N

W

S

Round Island

Sugar Island

Boblo Island

Hickory Island

Lake Erie

PROLOGUE

"Dad, can we stop at the 45th parallel sign and take a picture to remember our first road trip together?" fourteen-year-old, Wiley Davis asked. It was Sunday and they were just leaving Traverse City, Michigan.

"Sure." Detective Jack Davis laughed softly to himself as he turned on his signal and applied the brakes. He was happy to oblige. Off duty and relaxed after three days of exploring with his son and Dr. Linn Erickson, his significant other, he was touched Wiley thought enough about their time spent together to want a memento.

Leaving the car at the side of the road, the three trooped through scrub grass to stand between the metal legs of the sign. Captivated by its message, Wiley was insistent they all be in the shot.

45th PARALLEL
HALFWAY BETWEEN
EQUATOR & NORTH POLE

"Say cheese," a kind tourist coached without imagination after offering to take the picture.

"That was a great idea!" Linn exclaimed, when they were back in the car. Flashing Jack a smile, she turned around in her seat to look directly at Wiley.

"You're pleased with what you saw?"

"Very!" the teen replied with a wide grin. "It was better than I thought!"

The trip had been Linn's idea. In an unprecedented move, Wiley's father had agreed to it and engineered an excused absence for his son from school to go visit Northwestern Michigan College in Traverse City when Wiley had voiced an interest in their Great Lakes Water Studies Institute.

Since loading the car for the five hour trip home, Wiley had been a million miles away thinking about all he'd seen. From the moment he'd read about the school and what it offered, he hoped it could be the gateway to preparing him for his future. Even though he'd been excited to come, he hadn't thought the place would live up to his expectations.

He wanted to be a Freshwater Ranger. It was a title he'd made up. He envisioned patrolling the rivers and lakes of Michigan underwater in a mini-sub. To his knowledge, the job didn't really exist, nor did he see the role clearly. Some occupations, like being a member of the Coast Guard, came close to what he was thinking, but he was more interested in what was happening below the water than above, and saw himself as more of an independent agent versus a member of a vast, multi-layered organization. The one thing he was sure of was the planet's water needed protection if further generations of plants and animals were to exist.

Everything Wiley had seen and heard about research facilities, laboratories internships, a floatplane, and a variety of vessels including the T/S Northwestern known as a floating classroom appealed to him.

There were other schools in the U.S. where he could study water, but if you were talking *fresh water*, and that was *his* interest, how could anywhere else surpass what was available right here in his home state? Michigan was not called the Great Lakes State for nothing. Three quarters of its land mass was surrounded by water. Big water! Legend had it, no matter where you were in the state, you couldn't go more than six miles in any direction without running into a lake, river, pond or stream. With all this at hand, why would you go anywhere else?

In the course of three days, all Wiley had encountered confirmed he could make his future happen. A future of his own design, if he had the guts to try. Because of the gift of this visit from his father and Linn and all of what he'd learned, his previously nebulous dream now had shape. He could visualize the trajectory of steps he needed to take and the instant the journey had become clear in his mind, he'd challenged himself to go for it. It was no longer such a stretch to imagine getting from where he was to where he wanted to go.

They were a long way from home. Michigan was divided into two major land masses. The Lower Peninsula was shaped like a mitten and the Upper Peninsula looked like the head of a wolf. They were linked by the Mackinaw Bridge. Traverse City, the Cherry Capital of the World, was in the Lower Peninsula, but about as far north as you could go. It sat on Grand Traverse Bay on the west side of the state.

Ever since Labor Day so much about Wiley's world had changed—been rearranged—knocking him off balance for the longest time.

It was now the middle of November, almost Thanksgiving. The trees were bare, the color gone from the landscape, and snowflakes floated in the air. He was thankful for so many things: This trip, his father, Linn, and living on Grosse Ile. But bigger than all those blessings was that he'd survived his crushing breakup with Cameron.

What had saved him?

He owed his escape from despair and hope of a brighter future to his father and Linn. Yet, the past and the terrible mistakes he'd made since just before school started still haunted him. He remembered each and every foolish thing he did, and all it had cost him.

• • •

Survival changes everything.

It was the last of its kind.

Someone would have to pay.

• • •

1

TAKE A CHANCE ON ME

THURSDAY BEFORE LABOR DAY WEEKEND

"Come on, Cameron," Wiley oozed and schmoozed warmly when he called her around 11 a.m. "This is Labor Day weekend! Our last free one before school starts. We may not have many more chances to get out on the water. You know we'll have a blast. Are you really going to say no?"

She didn't say no. She said nothing.

"Well?"

"I'll think about it."

"Okay," he said, but he didn't understand.

He'd thought they'd patched up their problems just before eighth grade ended, then he'd barely seen her all summer. Why was she hesitating? Why wasn't she excited to see him?

If she was scared to go out in his boat because of the missing zombie, that he *could* understand. Last fall, a creature had haunted his house. The mental picture of the milky-skinned, cloudy-eyed monster could keep him up at night. Sander Firth, a Keeper of the Watch, had shot it. Yet the body had never been recovered off the dock at his house where it fell into the drink. Surely, the zombie must have been destroyed. There hadn't been a single sighting in close to three months. What was the problem?

"I have crew practice until five," he told her. "I'll call you later."

Wiley's thoughts swirled crazily after he hung up. He had met Cameron at the beginning of seventh grade in math class, back when she was two inches taller than he. They'd become friends, then something more. He loved the way she looked at him…when she did look at him, which lately wasn't very often.

She walked a different path than most of the girls he knew. 'My explorer,' she called him, when he dreamed out loud of what he could do as a Freshwater Ranger. Like the hot sun burning brightly above heavy cloud cover, the depth of Wiley's desire wasn't always on show. His cool demeanor kept it well hidden. He shared only what he cared about most with those who could understand. Like Cameron. She got it.

And better yet, she had her own ambitions. After enrolling in an eight-week computer science program, she'd enhanced her E-style so much, Wiley watched with fascination. Unlike so many adults, whose children's immersion into the tech-savvy world frightened them, Cameron's parents supported her interest and dedication. It didn't hurt that her father was into it too. He understood the powerful draw of designing algorithms to the exclusion of other pursuits, but an-all-or-nothing approach to anything wasn't healthy. Through his urging, Cameron tried to find a balance between her passion for coding and having a life.

Until recently, talking with Cameron about the future had been a blast. They agreed on practically everything, like using their talents to design a future to make their dreams come true. Work that turned you on was just a different kind of play.

Now however, Wiley was worried. Last year Cameron had been open, honest, and easy to talk to, but that had changed, and he didn't know why. For the first time, he was kind of looking forward to the start of a new school year. They were entering high school, and tomorrow was freshman orientation, meaning he'd probably see her. Maybe if the two of them shared some classes, they might reconnect in a good way.

As he ran around the house pulling together stuff he would need for practice, his confusion over Cameron's reaction didn't lessen, but his mood lightened. School for Wiley was not a first love, but he couldn't stop it from starting. There was some good news, though. Because of Labor Day, school started on Tuesday, meaning his first week would only be four days long!

Having found what he needed, he was standing by the road next to his garage when Brian Roberts' mother arrived to drive him to practice. Brian was Wiley's best friend.

The two boys, both tall, lanky brunettes, were almost always together so people often mistook them for twins. But they were very different. Brian sprinted through life, firing on and off as he tackled one thing after another in a big, easy, and happy burst of energy that left him spent by the end of each day.

Wiley was far less outgoing, directing his energy inward, releasing it in a long, steady burn. His dark, chocolate-brown eyes surveyed and summed up everything he encountered, leaving him slower to throw a smile than his green-eyed friend. And that was the beauty of their relationship. Brian's exuberance counterbalanced Wiley's brooding nature.

Home to both kids was a two-by-twelve mile stretch of about ten small islands, (lumped together and connected by bridges, some inhabited, some not, and at least one privately owned) called Grosse Ile. The Island, as it was referred to with a capital I, was located in southeast Michigan at the end of the Detroit River, where it opened into Lake Erie. Considered a boat-owner's paradise, Grosse Ile offered the convenience of civilization next to the beauty of the wild.

Wiley and Brian lived doors apart on the tiny, but uniquely laid out island of Hickory. The shoreline was ringed by houses to take advantage of the spectacular view, leaving the land in the center building free. The big, open expanse of grass was a luxurious space, much loved by those who lived around it.

After Wiley got in the car and they were on their way, Mrs. Roberts tried hard to pry details of their lives out of the teens. They answered readily, unconsciously filtering their answers to provide only enough scoop to satisfy her inquisition, and not give away anything incriminating.

Mrs. Roberts and Wiley's mother had been childhood playmates, and the best of friends, much like their sons. The four had been practically inseparable until Annie Davis died almost four years ago. Brian's mom had been a huge, comforting presence in Wiley's life as far back as he could remember. She still meant the world to him.

"Thanks for the ride," the boys called, when she dropped them off.

Mrs. Roberts smiled. "I'll be back!"

"Good!" They laughed and waved, before turning their backs and walking away.

"How are things between you and Cameron?" Brian asked, as soon as they were out of earshot of his mother.

"Fine," Wiley said, hoping to sound nonchalant. But he was uncomfortable about where this conversation might be headed.

"Everything's okay?"

"Yes, I just talked to her." Wiley swallowed hard and called his bluff. "Why?"

"If things are really all right, then you're lucky. Stevie Gail is just playing with you, man. Why else would an upper classman be hanging around a lowly freshman?"

Wiley stopped walking.

"I'm not interested in Stevie Gail," he said, but the tone of his voice gave him away. He couldn't resist asking, although he was afraid of Brian's answer. "You think Cameron cares?"

Brian's mouth dropped open, his face a mask of surprise. "Why do you think she's been so upset and you've seen so little of her?"

"Come on…Stevie's just fun."

"Uh huh," Brian commented dryly. He and Wiley had slowed their steps and were standing face to face in the parking lot. "That's not what it looks like. More like you can't resist the attention."

Wiley laughed, but he felt under attack. "Really, it's no big deal." His face had grown hot, his hands sweaty.

"That's bull and you know it! Stevie's trouble. Everyone's watching. Your enemies are hoping you make a huge fool out of yourself and go down in flames."

"I'm not going to do anything stupid, okay?"

"You're already doing stupid! Do you *really* think Cameron's going to put up with you sniffing around another girl?"

"Relax, Brian. Cameron knows she's the one. I'm not going to hurt her."

"Too late for that, you already broke her heart. If you keep acting like an ass, you'll crush her. Trust me."

"There's nothing going on with Stevie and me."

"I hope not, or you'll be sorry."

• • •

As soon as practice was over, Wiley texted Cameron.

<Can u talk?>

He wanted an answer from her about the weekend. But more than that, after being scolded by Brian he wanted to hear her voice and judge her mood for himself. Was Stevie Gail really the source of Cameron's aloofness?

<After dinner. 7:30?>

Pleased she'd responded and hadn't brushed him off, Wiley plunked down at the kitchen table and turned on the TV. He had an hour and a half to kill. He was startled when the back door opened and his father, Detective Jack Davis of the Grosse Ile Police, walked in carrying two bags of groceries. His father had recently traded shifts and now worked daylight. Wiley hadn't quite gotten used to the new arrangement.

"I got some great stuff for dinner. Shish kabobs for the grill and guess what's for dessert."

"Pie?" Wiley asked, ever hopeful. He punched off the TV, knowing television in general annoyed his dad.

"Peach."

"Excellent!"

"While I turn on the grill, why don't you make a list of things you'll need for Tuesday. The weekend will be more fun if you get as much as possible ready now. And remember, don't drink from the water fountains for a few days. Who knows how long the water has been sitting in the pipes."

Wiley nodded absently. Last year any advice would have made him cringe. But the atmosphere between father and son had swung from hostile to friendly this spring, when they both became entangled in what had become known as the Round Island Mystery.

"There's lunch money in an envelope on top of your dresser."

Food. Wiley had completely forgotten he'd need money to eat on Tuesday. "Thanks. I hope I get an early lunch period. Last year was torture."

"Yes, I bet. I've seen you eat."

His dad surprised him by leaving his preparations for dinner to come and sit at the table. "Boy, it seems like a million years ago I was in ninth grade. Our class got screwed. Right after they built the new high school, instead of our changing buildings and moving up, we had to stay an extra year at the junior high, as it used to be called. It made us crazy."

"Yeah?" Wiley knew very little about his dad's youth, besides he'd loved to play football. "I never really thought about it."

"You can't imagine. The old 1911 building was where your great-grandmother and various other family members slaved away for years. It's kind of sad they tore it down. I have lots of fond memories of the place. The outside was built of grey limestone which was soft, not hard like bricks, so students used one particular wall to etch declarations of love and boasts of grandeur. The classrooms had huge, double-hung windows allowing sunlight to flood in and offering stupendous views of the river beyond. The windows were the bane of every mind-numbing teacher, but were the salvation for most of us being held captive for fifty-some excruciating minutes."

Jack paused to pull his thoughts together. Then he barked a laugh.

"The inside of the building was made mostly of wood. A large metal shoot, similar to the emergency ones which inflate from airplanes, was permanently attached to the rear of a second story classroom as a fire escape."

"That's wild."

"It was. The teachers nagged us to death about it, saying it was 'off limits;' to be used 'only in an emergency.' If they'd quit harping, no one would have paid any attention. They just kept beating us over the head with warnings." His dad shook his head. "Any misconduct would carry a heavy penalty. It turned out that part was true."

"What happened?"

"During history class, Tony Leland accepted a bet and slid down to freedom, right in the middle of a lecture on how Arch Duke Ferdinand managed to get himself killed and start WWI. You could always count on Leland to do something outrageous. Tony loved breaking rules and bucking authority. He hated school."

"Did he get kicked out?"

"No, they suspended him for three days, which he loved. He viewed it as a holiday. The rest of us lost privileges for a week. The class of '69 had a terrible reputation. We were endlessly in trouble."

"*You* graduated in '69?" Wiley blurted.

"I did. And it was a long time ago."

Having finished his walk down memory lane, Wiley's father got up and went back to preparing dinner.

● ● ●

Cameron picked up after two rings.

"Tell me about your big plans," she said, with little enthusiasm.

Up until July, a rowboat had been Wiley's only means of getting around on the water. Then luck broke his way. A neighbor was selling his Boston Whaler to get a bigger ride. Was Wiley interested in the 110 Sport?

"It's the perfect starter powerboat," his neighbor said. "Whalers are legendary for being unsinkable. The motor is only twenty-five horsepower, so it will move you around without getting tricky."

It wasn't too hard to convince his father this was a good deal, and more to the point, he could handle the responsibility. Eventually, Wiley's dad agreed to pay half, and the teen covered the balance from saved birthday and holiday money. It would break him, but he didn't care.

The boat was small, only about twelve feet long and a bit cramped with four kids plus equipment, but it was his! Jack Davis's rowboat rules still applied: no solo outings and Lake Erie was totally off limits. Circling Hickory, and going across to Sugar Island were his to explore.

"Saturday morning," Wiley cajoled Cameron, "let's go and beach on the other side of Sugar. You've never been out in the Whaler, and I don't have to be back until afternoon to help with the party."

"I can't, I have a tennis lesson Saturday morning."

"Can you change it?"

"Probably not."

"What time is it?" Wiley tried next. "We can go after."

"I don't know how long I'll be, it might run over. I don't want to disappoint."

"*You* are still coming to the party, right?" Wiley asked, exasperated by her lack of interest and his inability to get her to agree.

"Yes," she laughed, pleased at hearing his worry. "My whole family's psyched."

"Okay." Happy she had warmed up a bit, he backed off. "Just know, if you change your mind the invitation is open."

But Wiley was thrown. He'd failed to talk her into going with him. Brian's warning echoed in his head. Had his friend been right? How could Cameron not know he cared about her, and only her? It's not like he'd been off kissing Stevie. That *would* be going too far.

Cameron called back an hour later.

"Does your dad know about you're plans?" she asked.

"Not yet, but how can he be against it?" Wiley's mind raced. What could he say to turn her no into a yes? "He's been out a few times this summer and we're only going to Sugar. We could be home in no time at any sign of danger."

"If he gives the green light, I'll go if Libby and Brian come too."

"Great! I'll clear it with my dad and ask Brian. What time works for you?"

"I can be at your house by 11:00 a.m."

"Perfect! See you tomorrow at orientation."

Next Wiley texted Brian.

<Want 2 go out Sat w Lib and Cam?>

<I'm in. Will ask Lib. Talk am>

Wiley went to bed a happy man.

2

FISHING FOR ANSWERS

THURSDAY BEFORE LABOR DAY WEEKEND

"Hey, Moreno," Rob Foley called wearily into his lapel mike. He was tired and hungry; it was close to 3:30 p.m. They'd been at this for a while.

"Yeah? What 'ya need?"

Foley's partner, J.T. Moreno was seated at the controls in the pilot house of the eighty foot fishing trawler. From the outside, the boat was a disgraceful looking thing. Worn paint, rusty patches, and old fishing nets littering the deck made it hardly worth anyone's attention. Or so they hoped. It had been recently reconfigured with exacting specifications to house their newest enterprise, and one they wished to remain unnoticed.

Standing near the stern, Foley frowned at a dial mounted on an intake valve. At thirty-three, the 5'9" spark plug of a man was in perfect health, except for an ever increasing waistline due to a love of beer. His slick, blue-black, wavy hair shone in the sunshine.

"We've got no suction. The pipe must be clogged," he relayed. Although the August sky was clear, foot-high swells rocked and rolled the surface of Lake Erie beneath him. "Turn up the power a few notches, and let's see if we can clear it without having to pull the whole thing up. That'll take forever and we're so exposed here I want to hurry, get finished, and get out."

"Hang on…," Moreno returned patiently from his perch. Six inches taller and two years younger than Foley, Moreno looked older thanks to the sprinkling of salt and pepper throughout his shortly cropped hair.

The power surge helped. Foley relaxed his tense muscles as the dial returned to normal and the sucking of water from the lake resumed. Besides draining him of energy, the sun beating down on his back was making him thirsty, which was rather ironic considering he was floating in the middle of Lake Erie, surrounded by miles and miles of fresh water. He'd been standing on deck for hours, but besides a few minor inconveniences he had no real complaints. On this fine day, he and his partner were having the time of their lives stealing water from a seemingly inexhaustible source—a Great Lake. They would deliver it, for a tidy profit, to the French corporation, Océane Industries.

The future was all about water. And Océane wanted it. All of it!

Unbeknownst to local authorities, Océane, well known in Michigan for solving many of the state's overwhelming water pollution issues, was also busy breaking one of its newest regulations.

At a Governors' Convention made up of the eight states (Minnesota, Wisconsin, Illinois, Indiana, Ohio, Michigan, Pennsylvania, and New York) and the two Canadian provinces (Quebec and Ontario) that bordered the Great Lakes, a law was enacted prohibiting the divergence of huge amounts of fresh water to protect already record-low lake levels. In a region suffering from the domino effect of a failed American auto industry and its associated businesses, any further loss in revenue from ventures dependent on water, like fishing, electrical power, tourism, and shipping would make a bad situation worse. Even drink companies were feeling the pinch of the rising price of their basic ingredient, forcing them to find creative ways to curb their usage.

To their credit, Océane Industries tried, but failed, to get governmental permission to drain off a steady stream of Lake Erie. But the enormous volume of water was irresistible to Océane, who knew its worth. With so much of the world desperate for water, the Great Lakes could no longer be viewed as just part of the landscape. Its value had shifted from something pretty to look at or fun to use recreationally, to housing a commodity worth a fortune. Océane, recognizing an easy opportunity to quadruple its U.S.

earnings, was deep in the thick of it.

Moreno and Foley were hired. They happily reconverted their fishing trawler to hold a different kind of catch. Each day they delivered thousands of gallons of the liquid gold to the company freighter, Océane II. From there the water was transported to a bottling plant in Detroit, then shipped and sold to states and countries desperate to hydrate their ever increasing and unstoppable population growth.

Suddenly, the pitch of the trawler's well-oiled, well-tuned motor turned to a whine. Checking the dial on the water intake valve, Foley discovered it had bounced all the way to the left, indicating the flow of water from lake to boat was down to a trickle.

"Aw heck, something's stuck fast," Foley radioed tensely. "Turn off the engine before it burns up. I'm gonna pull it up and check it out."

"Right," Moreno bellowed back.

As the engine's roar died, Foley pushed a button marked with an up arrow on the control panel of the crane towering above him. Almost soundlessly, gears engaged and a thick cable wire that snaked down into the blue-green water began to spool backwards, wrapping itself neatly around a huge drum. Attached to the cable was a six-inch wide, white plastic tube used to draw up the lake water and send it below deck into one of two huge holding tanks.

Up until this moment, Foley and Moreno's new collaboration had come together effortlessly. From meeting with the executives of Océane Industries to buying and refurbishing the boat, things had gone so smoothly that just this morning Foley had asked his partner if life could get much better. Two months ago, each of them had been scraping together a living that provided less than the basics. After joining forces, both their lives and incomes changed dramatically. For them, crime was beginning to pay. And pay big.

"What now?" Foley asked, completely mystified.

The cable wire, which was attached to the vacuum pipe, had quit retracting. Taut as a violin string, it shuddered violently as the winch strained to pull it and the pipe out of the water.

Before real damage occurred to the expensive equipment, Foley slammed his palm on a big red stop button. Speculating on what to do next, he was amazed and delighted when the wire jerked hard and then laid still. Spring-ing forward, he hit the green button and the winch resumed retracting. He heaved a great sigh of relief. The problem seemed to have fixed itself.

As the plastic pipe cleared the deck, Foley guided it with the palm of his hand to keep it from snagging on the edge of the boat.

"Holy moly," he cried, as the end finally emerged from down under. "Moreno," he called into his mike. Slapping his hand against the stop but-ton once again he urged, "You better come here!"

"What's wrong now?"

"You gotta see this. We almost caught something and it was no fish!"

Split and frayed, the opening of the pipe looked like it had been blown apart by a firecracker.

"Oh sure!" Moreno mocked. "Maybe it was a mermaid!" The more cau-tious of the two, the tall, fit, thirty-one-year-old rarely fell for more than half of what his excitable partner told him. Leaning back in his seat, Moreno wiped his brow with his sleeve. Even with tinted windows, the glass box in which he sat was getting hot. "You *do* realize," Moreno continued, "there are still a few king salmon in this lake."

"This was no fish," Foley insisted. "It had to have weighed a heck of a lot more than a salmon! You've gotta see it!"

"Okay, okay, hold your horses. I'm on my way."

This was their second haul of the day. They had decided to try and gath-er a morning and afternoon load, breaking Océane's rule of only one per day. Too much time on the water increased their exposure and the risk of being caught by satellite. However, just this once, by doubling their take they could meet their goal plus have Monday, a national holiday, off. Foley couldn't understand why they should have to ask for permission. Shouldn't a laborer have a relaxing Labor Day? How could their employer not think that was okay?

"Wow, would 'ya look at that!" Moreno exclaimed, when he finally saw the end of the pipe. "The plastic burst open like it was made of paper!"

"It's supposedly shred proof." Bending closer, Foley ran his fingers over the frayed material. "Something got stuck fast and managed to escape by popping the tubing wide open!"

"Yeah, what could *do* that? What's *down* there?" Moreno wondered aloud.

He scanned the endless horizon, seeing only water in all directions. The vast emptiness, whose isolation usually brought him comfort, suddenly felt threatening. They were so exposed, their only protection was the trawler. A shiver of fear ran the length of his spine, in spite of a brilliant blue sky.

"Don't know, but I've got an idea," Foley grinned slyly. "Let's try and catch it!"

"Are you kidding?" Moreno's insides churned at the thought. "Why? It'd be a total waste of time because whatever it is, it's gotta be long gone." Sometimes, if he poked enough holes in Foley's idiotic inspirations, his partner would lose interest and forget about it. But Moreno loved puzzles, so he couldn't help but ask, "Anyway, just how would you propose we capture it?"

"Yeah, okay…let me think."

Totally enthralled, Foley turned his focus to figuring out the logistics of putting his plan into action.

They'd chosen to come to this part of Lake Erie intentionally as another way to escape notice. Labeled a Dead Zone by the Environmental Protection Agency, the area was a toxic hot spot. No one, if they were at all cognizant of current environmental issues, came here. During the last few months, far down under the magnificent surface of the water the hot summer sun had kindled a cocktail of death.

When the sun warmed the water and its temperature rose, oxygen was depleted. Without the O making up H_2O, the most desirable species of plants and fish died in the hostile environment. However, unwanted invaders like zebra and quagga mussels, arriving in bilge water of freighters from foreign countries, liked the conditions and multiplied voraciously. With only a twenty-four hour life cycle, their remains quickly piled up on the lakebed. The huge amounts of accumulated waste putrefied, further poisoning the water. Hordes of bird and fish carcasses routinely washed up on the shores, if they were unlucky enough to eat from the area. Humans found the loss of so much wildlife heartbreaking, but their distress over a summer phenomenon faded during winter when all their energy shifted to dealing with snow and ice. Therefore, getting a complex problem like a Dead Zone completely resolved never quite happened.

"Look, there it is! That's what got caught in our pipe!" Foley shouted. A flash of white broke the surface about twenty feet out.

"Get a load of the size!" Moreno was transfixed. Mimicking a dolphin, the unidentified visitor was doing tricks, diving into and out of the water and rolling over and over as though trying to be seen. "Why in the world is it hanging around here after getting caught in the pipe?"

"It must want something."

"From us?" Moreno shrieked.

"Why else?"

"Dream on…" Rattled by the quick turn of events, Moreno jumped as a loud thud reverberated beneath their feet. "What the…?"

"It's ramming the hull to get our attention."

"Well, it worked! What the heck could it want with *us*? This whole thing's crazy!"

"What if we trimmed off the broken end," Foley said, ignoring his partner's distress, "of the suction tubing, and used it to suck this thing up again?"

"Nah," Moreno answered almost at once, intrigued again. Even with his stomach clenched in fear, his imagination was off and running. "The chances of that happening twice are lousy. It will avoid what trapped it. You need some kind of bait. But who knows what would attract the thing."

"Bait, huh…"

"Or there's that thick plastic mesh in the hold," Moreno said, testing his idea out loud.

"That's good. We can rig a net out of the mesh, like a drawstring bag and troll for the thing! We'll double the thickness for added strength, and place small weights at the closed end so it will sink. The net can hang from the crane, then we'll drop it in the water out where the thing is swimming. We'll pull the net along behind us, and if we make the opening nice and wide, the creature might get snagged and it'll be ours!"

"But why do we want it?" Moreno shook his head in confusion. His interest of the thing was only in solving the 'how to'—the production puzzle.

"It's valuable, if only for its freak factor!"

Moreno was the one freaked, but he helped gather the needed supplies. Spreading everything out on deck, it took about twenty-five minutes to construct their invention. As they worked, the creature circled, jumping out of the lake periodically as a reminder it was still there.

"Okay, here goes." Crazed with excitement, Foley lowered their trap into the water. Within minutes the cable line bounced wildly. "We got it!" he shouted.

Moreno stood speechless.

"Crank up the power," Foley ordered. "Let's pull it in, or it'll be history."

The crane clunked and squealed as the cable recoiled. When their newly won treasure broke the surface, Moreno hit the stop button allowing the bright orange netting to dangle over the water. As it swung back and forth in the air, water drained off a big white, rather human-looking body. It thrashed and squirmed, trying its best to break free. The men stared in wonder.

"Okay, Moreno, turn the crane back on and pull it closer."

The crane brought the bouncing bag towards them, along with a hideous odor.

"Yikes!" Moreno slapped his left hand over his nose and mouth, and hit the stop button with his right.

Two eyes, cloudy in ruin, peered at them through the mesh.

"Hang on, hang on," Foley said. "The thing's lying still now, but let's not take any chances. I'm gonna get some bungee cords, and lace them through the holes in the mesh to straitjacket the arms and legs around the body. That way it can't break out."

Moreno had no reply. He could only stare.

When Foley returned, both men cautiously approached the bag from either side. As they got closer, the noxious odor made them gag.

"What's slathered all over it?" Moreno turned his head to the side and sucked in big gulps of air.

"Some kind of gel." Foley, was holding the bottom of his T-shirt over his mouth and nose. "Better not touch it."

"Fat chance! I'm getting gloves."

"Grab me a pair, will 'ya?"

Finally, they lowered the bag onto the deck. The creature, heavily co-cooned in the elastic cords, resembled a Christmas tree ready for transport.

"What the heck is it?" Moreno breathed deeply.

Their catch looked like a man—and yet it didn't. Lying still, flat on its back, its facial features portrayed no emotion. Large, bulging, black eyes, weeping yellow trails of mucus, stared up unblinkingly at the sun. Clothed in a black wetsuit which had seen better days, the massive body was just about six feet in length. There was a huge hole in one of its shoulders. The exposed skin of its hands, feet, and face appeared bluish-white, like the color of skim milk. Smeared all over it was a clear salve that shimmered in the bright sunlight. It covered, but didn't hide several nasty ruptures.

"We've scored big time! It's the missing zombie!" Foley was jubilant. Ignoring his wooziness from the stench, he crouched closer to the prone body. "Remember last fall there was that huge ruckus on Grosse Ile about the last two zombies in the world being shot on that detective's dock? Both bodies fell into the lake, but later it was reported only one was recovered.

Here is the other, the one that got away! And now it's *ours!*"

"I don't want it. It's hideous!" Moreno whispered. Scrutinizing the thing's bloodless pallor and its remarkably still chest, he instructed, "Get rid of it. Throw it back in! See...it's not moving. I think we killed it by pulling it out of the water." Aware his mouth was salivating heavily; Moreno moved to the railing and spit over the side. Maintaining his distance, he reiterated, "No way it's still alive."

"What do you mean alive?" Foley barked a laugh, removed his soaked ball cap, and ran his other hand through his matted hair. Drops of sweat dotted his upper lip. "Moreno, you don't seem to get it. A living zombie? Isn't that an oxymoron?"

3

STILL IN THE GAME

FRIDAY, LABOR DAY WEEKEND

"It was ours in the first place," Claire Barrett told him, like a petulant child. "Frieda and Ernst Karlsson created those zombies *exclusively* for us! The undead were the perfect tool to sabotage water-related problems so we could get more work here in the U.S. They can swim in toxicity that would kill a human! By using them to wreak havoc we knew in advance which communities would be screaming for someone to please come and fix their problem so they could take a shower. We were the first company on the scene, with the perfect remedy to fix their woes. Because of the *zombies* our workload increased, we made gobs of money, and Océane's reputation as the # 1 water problem solver in the world went viral, *remember*?"

Claire was in no mood to suffer fools. These days, Niles Beauchamp, her CFO and partner at Océane Industries, was exactly that. He'd lost his edge.

The two Océane executives had just arrived in Michigan on their private jet from their headquarters in France. Their gentle touchdown put them into their slot at the Executive Terminal at 3:23 p.m. The place was a mob scene. People, who could afford to travel by private plane, were scrambling to get to their dream destination to enjoy the Labor Day Weekend.

Claire was wide awake; she rarely felt the effects of jetlag. "Here, read." She shoved her iPhone in Niles's face.

<Drone surveillance last 48 hrs found no proof one way or the other creature still functioning. FSH>

Niles felt bile rise in his throat. "Who is FSH?"

"Another set of eyes keeping tabs for us here in Michigan."

Us. Right.

"You're wasting money on a drone to look for a zombie that hasn't been seen since it was shot three months ago?" he questioned further.

Niles fought to keep his composure. He was furious, but not entirely sure why. Was it because she hadn't told him this before? Or was it the fact she would not give up chasing disaster?

"After seeing how badly it all ended," he said, probing for a reaction so she would tell him more, "you're still pursuing the walking dead? We don't need it any longer! We've become rich and Océane wields great power. What would you do with a reanimation, Claire? Possess it like a trophy, or worship it as an idol?"

Nile's words cut Claire like a knife, but she shook it off. He was no longer a believer. He'd become complacent with all the money they'd earned. She couldn't afford to let him distract her.

"Call me curious," she told him with a shrug. "It remains an unknown, having never been recovered. Like lost treasure."

"How exactly do Foley and Moreno play into this plan?"

"They're on Lake Erie every day stealing water for us," Claire said. "Why shouldn't they search for the creature at the same time? If they see it, they can pick it up."

As the plane's cabin door opened, Claire rose gracefully from her seat and grabbed her briefcase. All sixty-seven inches of her magnificent body, enhanced with every conceivable surgery, dye job, or other beauty enhancement available, were perfectly groomed. She looked, and was, in total control.

"Foley and Moreno are in our employ, doing our bidding," she continued to remind her partner. "We can ask anything of them. To get what we want, all we have to do is provide clear instructions on how to handle such a situation if it were to arise."

Claire could barely believe Niles had once been one of the few people she liked. Maybe even her favorite. Today she barely recognized him. His closed-off, scared little thoughts bored her. The events they'd suffered through together in the last year had changed him. He'd gone so far as to demand she promise not to get involved with a woman named Heidi Beyer. Niles had never threatened her before, and it had not pleased her. To make him back off, she'd done as he asked and promised to not see Heidi. Then she'd met with her anyway. Claire would do anything to insure Océane Industries remained safe and profitable. That included meeting with toxic Heidi Beyer, the original—and only—owner of the coveted secret: How to bring the dead back to life.

Since last spring both she and Niles had held their breath to see if their involvement with the Karlssons would be discovered. Scientists Frieda and Ernst Karlsson, understanding a zombie's value, had found a way to make Heidi Beyer talk and hand over her treasured secret to them.

When Ernst had come to Océane Industries seeking financing to begin experimentation, the two Océane executives said yes. That decision had brought Claire and Niles fame and fortune. But there was a dark side. If their association ever became known, Océane would be blacklisted by most of humanity who loathed the idea of zombies, and they would lose *everything* she and Niles had worked for during the last two decades.

They'd escaped ruin so far. The experience had damaged Niles, draining him of his taste for power, and leaving Claire wondering how to get rid of him.

So be it, she thought. *Not everyone makes it into your future, no matter how important they may have been in the past.*

"Our previous involvement with these monsters was hardly worth the despair," Niles said.

"I disagree," Claire practically spat. She was sick of the subject. Fighting to remain civil, she said, "Have you forgotten we are where we are now, thanks to their ministrations?"

"I haven't forgotten a thing," he hissed. "I remember it *all* very clearly… and I'm ashamed we sank so low as to use sabotage to gain profitability."

"Come on, you know it was about more than numbers! What happened to our dreaming about what these things could do, if given half a chance?"

she cried in exasperation.

"I've gotten stuck on what they *did* do like going rogue and killing people."

"It was bad, I know…but look at our gain," she championed. "Océane has been crowned king!"

"Exactly. Don't put it at risk."

Claire bristled at his insinuation *she* might cause the company's demise by pushing forward. What could hurt them far more, in her opinion, was Niles and his 'do nothing' attitude. Unable to contain herself any longer, she blasted him. "Business as usual has become blah. I want more." After deplaning, Claire stepped onto the tarmac and waited for her partner, who was right behind her.

Niles stopped at her side, closed his eyes, and raised his face to the sky. He was not going to let Claire ruin everything. Right now, he was delighted to be un-cooped and outside. But feeling her hand on his arm, her steely grip reminded him he needed to be very careful. He opened his eyes to find Claire staring at him with a touch of defiance, her unconcealed pride in what she'd achieved, with or without him, fully on display.

"We currently *lead* the industry," she said, her voice low and authoritative. "The next stage is to *own* the industry. Create a monopoly. And that means grabbing and controlling distribution."

As she entered the terminal, Claire considered what to do about this 'new' Niles. Together for almost twenty years, they'd lived and breathed Océane Industries. Their baby had grown into a remarkable young adult, poised to conquer the world. If she and Niles no longer wanted the same things, then, what was her next move?

After they cleared customs and could talk together again, Claire pulled him to the side. She had more to say, but it needed to be done in private.

"Clean water," she told him, "fit enough to sustain life, is disappearing fast. People refuse to believe it's happening, making it the *perfect* time to sneak in and take control. I'll use any means possible to do it."

"If Foley and Moreno were to catch the zombie," Niles said, interrupting her, "how do you plan to keep it without the whole world knowing?"

His question, a good one, caught her off guard.

"Why not advertise we have it?" she threw out. "The public sees it as the enemy. We can make a big deal out of pretending to destroy it, thus becoming exalted heroes. This is a great way, along with the donations we've poured into keeping Asian carp out of the Great Lakes, to present ourselves as the good guys who fight seriously scary water monsters."

Niles was impressed with her quick thinking, if not with the idea.

"Tell me. What else has drawn you back to Michigan?"

"This state is so crippled," she said quickly, her growing enthusiasm evident as she gave thought to his question, "thanks to a string of corrupt politicians who have financially bled it dry. It's ripe for takeover, and a perfect opportunity has presented itself for us to step in and fix it."

"Which is?" At hearing Claire had a proposal, Niles felt a faint spark of interest ignite within him. She could be brilliant at times, when she wasn't distracted by things like zombies.

"Since the algae bloom infestation this July in Toledo, Ohio, forced the city to declare its water unsuitable to drink, pollution personally touched a city of 500,000. Public awareness is now on our side. Because of a tainted water supply, people couldn't bathe, use ice from ice makers, or swim in their pools right in the middle of summer!"

"Toledo's only a little more than an hour's drive from Detroit," Niles said, thoughtfully.

"More luck for us! If Detroit residents weren't nervous before about delivery and water quality, they're scared now," Claire said. "Both cities draw at least some of their water from the same source: Lake Erie.

"Here's my idea. In 2006, Detroit Water and Sewage used federal money to build a fabulous facility to evaluate the purity of water pulled from Lake Erie and Lake Huron, before sending it out to more than a million customers. To their surprise, operating the new machinery proved very expensive, and far pricier than their budget allows. Currently, Detroit can't cover the cost of running the system. But they don't *dare* not test the water!"

Niles nodded. "Michigan's citizens are screaming about exorbitant utility rates. They won't stand for another increase." Niles found himself smiling in spite of the tension between them. "And U.S. law dictates clean water must be provided to all citizens."

"Exactly," Claire said. "People have become spoiled after receiving a seemingly endless supply of cheap, drinkable water for decades. The predicament in Toledo was a huge wakeup call for what the future may hold. Especially as the algae bloom incident happened in July, almost *two months* earlier than September when conditions are at their peak for this type of water disaster."

"How does this affect Océane?" Niles questioned.

Claire was pleased. This was the old Niles talking, one captivated by how they could outfox their competitors. "What's the one thing Océane has that Detroit lacks?" She didn't give him time to answer. "Money! I propose we offer the Motor City a contract to have Océane monitor their water quality at a bargain price."

"An offer they can't refuse."

"And we'll keep chipping away until we own the market!" Claire was jubilant. Here was the fun she'd been missing these last few months. Niles was acting interested, playing her game.

"Those frightened Toledo residents," she continued, "drove for miles, desperate to find clean water. They paid whatever was charged, no matter how outrageous the price. Eventually, I want the people of Michigan on their knees—just like the residents of Toledo—paying us top dollar to quench their thirst."

"Will that quench yours?" Niles asked shrewdly. "This is a smart plan, Claire. We can easily put together a promotional announcement and present it while we're in Michigan. See? We don't need a zombie! Our creative genius is a far superior tool."

"I think a variety of tools is best," she said wisely. "The fact that a zombie can swim in sewage makes it a valued resource. Foley and Moreno, our bottom-feeder meth makers, were trying to make a living cooking and selling junk from a tricked-out cabin cruiser when we hired them. These guys are dilettantes, amateurs who skim the surface of life without digging in and mastering anything. Because of our money, they aren't having to struggle so hard and they like it. Money is the key to unlocking their interest and loyalty. We pay them extremely well for harvesting water. I want them to know they will be paid *handsomely* if they bring us the creature."

"Claire, the zombie is as toxic as Toledo's algae-bloom water. You've just presented a brilliant design to bring us closer to our goal. Surely, we can conceive of other, equally ingenious ideas without messing with disaster."

"We can, and we will. But our having a reanimated being—if it's out there—is better than having someone else possess it." She searched his face, then shrugged after finding nothing of interest. "Even you once thought zombies held great promise."

"That was long before I understood the evil truth. That *thing* exists because someone dabbled in the blackest of arts. For that reason alone, we should stay clear."

"I know the dangers and it did nearly ruin everything for us." Rewarding him with one of her infrequent smiles, she added, "Let's just see what happens."

• • •

Waiting and seeing appeared to be the best deal Niles was going to get, at least for now. He knew Claire was shutting him out. Having worked together day and night for the last several years, he understood her better than anyone else on earth. He also knew she was heading down a path of destruction, whether she wanted to hear about it from him or not.

To regain his power standing with her, he needed to make a score bigger and better than any of hers. Her Detroit plan was clever. So far this morning, an opportunity for him to shine had not presented itself, but that was okay. He would remain in a state of alertness. His time would come, and he would be ready.

• • •

After their conversation, they boarded a Koala helicopter owned by Océane, and took to the air again. Their flight path went directly over Grosse Ile into Lake Erie airspace.

Their 740-foot freighter, Océane II, was running at ten knots heading away from Michigan toward Ohio. The ship was new, a beauty, and classified as a 'saltie'. It was just the right length to allow it to travel from the Atlantic Ocean through the locks of the St. Lawrence Seaway—the gateway to the Great Lakes. The pilot house and cabins were pristine, furnished with the latest equipment, and beautifully appointed. The helicopter circled, then made a soft landing on top of one of the loading bays that doubled as a landing site. The two owners stepped down from their flying machine onto the expansive deck.

"Have Foley and Moreno delivered their supply of water today?" Claire asked the captain, when they met with him in the pilot house.

"Yes. They've made two."

"Why two?" Claire frowned, clearly unhappy with the news.

The captain smiled charmingly, sensing trouble. "They don't want to work on Monday, Labor Day, so they're collecting extra in advance. We are to reconvene tomorrow, ETA at 10:00 a.m. Your cabins are ready," he told them hurriedly. He had no interest in getting in the middle of whatever was going on regarding the new delivery arrangements. He had enough to tend to, doing his real job. "The chef is preparing all you requested. Dinner will be served at seven. Will you join me on the bridge at six for cocktails? The sunset should be spectacular."

"Thank you. Six o'clock. We'll be there." Claire turned on her heels and headed to her cabin to shower and change.

Niles, still running silent, followed her lead.

4

PARTY PLANS

Wiley and Brian rode their bikes to the high school for orientation. Wiley made it through the arduous hours in fairly good shape. He'd seen Cameron, but not talked with her. There had been some good laughs with Brian and some others, and he'd managed to avoid nasty McKnight and his torturous gang. As he'd suspected, there was lots of new, new, new to get used to: a locker and combination to remember, a heavy class schedule that had him running all over the place, and a long list of rules he thought ridiculous.

Now, he needed to hustle. He had just a few minutes to get to the locker room and change his cloths before crew practice. This frantic pace and the long hours would take some getting used to again, after the summer's slower pace.

His stomach gurgled loudly. Without losing stride, he slipped the strap of his backpack from his shoulder and rummaged around inside until his hand closed on a Nutri-Grain bar. After readjusting his pack, he tore the package with his teeth and practically inhaled the contents.

Exhaustion surprised, and then threatened to undo him when he sat down to put on his shoes after changing into his practice clothes. Only the arrival of three of his teammates kept him operational. A combination of pushing and cajoling got him outside to catch the bus to the boathouse. He wished there was a way to skip practice and start his weekend a little sooner, but then the sugar he'd consumed from the power bar hit his system and he perked up. Soon he was laughing as one after another of the teens tried to out joke the other. The next thing he knew he was seated in an eight and out on the water.

• • •

Practice ended early. Wiley rode home trying not to think about food, focusing instead on how to get his dad to let him take his boat out tomorrow.

"Not again!" he muttered, as he barged through the back door, home at last. The animated conversation he'd heard coming from the kitchen had stopped abruptly, then hurriedly resumed in an awkwardly different direction.

Get over it, people! Did they really think he didn't notice?

Safely inside, he slipped off his backpack and let it fall to the floor. Setting down the huge sports bag he was lugging, he locked the door and reset the alarm.

"Hey, boy."

Parker, his nine-year-old mutt, wiggled and wagged his bushy tail in greeting. Wiley patted him absentmindedly, ignored his backpack, but picked up the athletic bag. Then, boy and dog gravitated toward the action in the kitchen.

As soon as Wiley poked his head into the room, the three adults seated at a round oak table decorated with a spread of drinks and hors d'oeuvres looked up guiltily, but greeted him warmly. Slouching against the door jam, Wiley's long and lean body sagged comfortably as he shed the pressure of the outside world. He surveyed the room full of adults with pleasure, glad to be home and among those he loved.

"Hey Linn, Steve, Dad, something smells good!" he sniffed appreciatively. "What's for dinner?"

Catching the look on his father's face, Wiley knew he was hiding something. Tight, worry lines pulled at his eyes and his lips were turned down in a scowl. The teen felt the exclusion, but was at a loss as to how to fix it.

"We're having grilled walleye with toasted almonds," his father said, "spinach salad with Feta cheese and lemon dressing, and eggplant casserole accompanied by homemade biscuits. For dessert there's chocolate cake."

"How soon?" Wiley asked.

"Soon."

The group conversation resumed, picked up momentum, and began to buzz. Teasing was prevalent, jokes were in excess. Happiness exuded from the group as they examined lists of all kinds that littered the kitchen table. They were in the midst of final preparations to ensure their joint Labor Day party was a success.

"How was practice? Did you row your guts out?" his father's partner, Steve Anderson, asked with a smile.

Steve and Wiley's dad were detectives and partners on Grosse Ile's police force. Over the years their relationship as trusted colleagues had morphed into a tight friendship. Being able to fully rely on each other was essential as they spent much of each waking day chasing down drug runners who found this quaint area a perfect location for their escalating trade.

"Not today," Wiley laughed. "We took the eight around the Island at a leisurely pace. People honked and waved at us from East River."

"Adulation for the team supreme," Steve teased. "After kicking serious butt last year rowing is now hot. Or is it just you?"

"Oh, for sure," Wiley shot right back with a big, fat smirk, "it's all about me."

At the beginning of seventh grade, Wiley made the decision to join the crew team instead of playing his father's beloved sport: football. Jack Davis, already simmering with unhappiness since the death of Wiley's mother, Annie, had been irked beyond reason by his refusal. His father's reaction to his son's choice of sport at first strained, and then almost killed their relationship.

Then, last Memorial Day weekend, a massacre in the kitchen of a house on Kelleys Island in Lake Erie blew everything wide open. It was discovered scientists Frieda and Ernst Karlsson owned the structure. They had built a well-hidden laboratory in the basement. The Karlssons also owned a house on Grosse Ile where they posed as an unassuming, married couple named Roth. From these secret labs they were creating the undead. They were running a zombie farm!

Wiley was the first to spot the vile, reanimated creatures from his living room window. They were swimming past his house on Hickory, going up the Detroit River. Eventually, in a showdown with the police at the scientists' Grosse Ile location, pandemonium and carnage prevailed. The Karlssons/Roths were killed and Wiley's father, mauled by a zombie, almost died. Surgeon Linn Erickson saved his life, and over the two weeks of his convalescence in the hospital she became a part of Jack and Wiley's world.

Hanging by their door was a poem given to father and son by Linn when Jack was released from the hospital. Wiley actually liked it.

The ordeal of waiting to see if Jack Davis would live or die had been horrendous for Wiley. Since the death of his mother, his relationship with his father had failed to thrive. The ambiance and joy previously abundant in their home slowly died too. Miraculously, as his dad recovered, so did their relationship. Long lost happiness bloomed once again at home and friends were welcome.

THIS HOUSE IS YOURS
This house is yours. Its portals open wide
And welcome you to all inside.
Dear friend and guest, enter in peace and rest.
This house is yours.

"At least you got out on the water," Steve said, jumping back into the conversation.

"Yes. It felt great!"

Opening the basement door, Wiley tossed his athletic bag down the steps where it landed with a loud smack. Quickly closing the door, he crossed the kitchen, opened the refrigerator, and pulled out a can of pop. The top hissed when he popped the tab as he came toward the adults. After joining them at the table, he took a big sip.

"Anything you need me to do?" he offered.

His father frowned slightly at the soda, but skipped the lecture he would have given in the past. Wiley's well-toned, well-preserved parent found it sickening so many adults fed their children drinks filled with empty calories. To him, excess calories coupled with little or no exercise was not a pretty sight.

Instead of harping, Jack rose from his seat and placed an easy hand on his son's shoulder. "There's nothing to do at the moment. Sit here, I'll get another chair. We're finalizing plans which reminds me, you need to cut the lawn and rake the shoreline for debris."

Over the past twelve months the water level in Lake Erie had steadily decreased. Plastic water bottles, drink cans, and other rubbish kept washing up in front of their house. It was an ugly sight and it drove Jack crazy.

"No problem, I was planning on doing it right after dinner." Wiping his palms on his jeans, the boy scooped up a handful of nuts and settled back in the chair. "Cameron, Brian, Libby and I are thinking about going out in my boat tomorrow morning."

"Do you think that's wise?" As the first responder to his announcement, Linn sounded curious, not critical. "We've gone so far as to hire guards for the party. Isn't going out in a boat tempting fate?"

Wiley smiled to himself. He'd been right. The group's supposedly relaxed atmosphere when he came home was nothing more than a temporary ruse. Without knowing what she was doing, Linn told him all he wanted to know. The adults were no longer talking zombie in front of him.

IF it still existed.

It had been three months with no sighting—an eternity!

Everyone was making a big deal out of nothing. It was a miracle they were having a party. But even Detective Jack Davis was tired of being cautious. It was his idea to host a real blowout with Linn, Steve, and Steve's girlfriend, Bridget Alexander, and invite everyone they knew. Initially, his plan was greeted with mixed reviews. No one could argue that the Davis yard was the perfect setting. Although not a huge plot of land, the lawn rolled gently down to the banks of the Detroit River and the view was stupendous. Uninhabited Sugar Island sat majestically about four hundred yards offshore. If that wasn't spectacular enough, here was where the Detroit River came to an end and Lake Erie opened wide, spreading south as far as the eye could see.

No one could forget this idyllic spot was also where the last two creations of scientists Frieda and Ernst Karlsson/Roth came out of the water onto the Davis' dock intent on destruction. They had gone rogue and stopped obeying commands. Sander Firth, a Keeper of the Watch, saved the day by blasting them back into the river. The human relief from those present was sigh-worthy. The terrible strain of waiting and watching for these unaccounted creatures to re-emerge and possibly inflict horrific damage to mankind was over.

Except, when their watery grave was dragged for bodies, only one was recovered. The fate of the other remained unknown; hence the ongoing worry for the party planners. If the thing was active…if it came after them—which if the first was true, then the second was likely—having it crawl out of the water during the festivities would be a disaster. Off-duty police officers from the surrounding communities had been hired to guard the shoreline so the guests could relax, mingle, and enjoy the setting.

Wiley knew the adults' unwillingness to talk in front of him about the danger was meant to protect him, and he appreciated their concern. But he'd rather be in on the conversation. From Linn's comment he suspected it was the female influence in this newly formed group that was pushing the agenda. Before women were involved, the two detectives were pretty forthcoming with facts, rarely shielding him from the worst details. If Linn and Bridget were the reason, Wiley was more than willing to put up with it. Getting mad seemed pointless, considering all the plusses the two brought into his life. It wasn't as though everyone was flat-out lying; they were just shielding him. Truth be told, thoughts of a renegade zombie were pretty disturbing. His dreams could prove it.

However, none of this introspection was as important as getting permission to use his boat tomorrow. Linn's concern played right into his hands. All he had to do was state his case.

"We are just going to Sugar," he replied easily. "We'll beach there and be back early so I can help with the party setup."

"You can go." Apparently Wiley's father needed no convincing. "But be back no later than 3 p.m. People have been invited for 5 p.m."

"Thanks. We'll be on time, I promise!" Trying to hide how pumped he was over getting the green light, Wiley looked around the table and smiled at each adult. "What's the R.S.V.P. outcome? Are lots of people coming?"

"Yes." Linn smiled back warmly. "Everyone has accepted: grandparents, parents, and all the friends you invited!"

"Kids are coming to this party?" Bridget joked, as she breezed into the room. An intensive care nurse, she'd met Steve when Jack had landed in the hospital during the Round Island Mystery. Walking up behind Wiley, she squeezed his shoulders. "Hey, when does school start?"

"Tuesday," he said, blushing with pleasure at the attention.

Next, Bridget beamed her high watt smile at Linn before moving around the table to give Steve a kiss. "Hey, handsome."

"Good, you got away." Steve rose to give her his seat. "No big holiday disasters, huh?"

"Not yet. The emergency room was so quiet it was spooky. Pray it stays that way and I don't get called in." As she sat down, she addressed the table. "Where are you in the discussion? Can I help?"

"Don't worry," Linn joked. "We have a list started for you."

"Bridget," Jack interrupted, "how about a drink to start off the holiday?"

"Yes, please, kind sir. I'm so ready to chill!"

"I'll get it for her, Jack," Steve said. "Anyone else ready for a new one?"

Jack began to gather empty cans, bottles, and dishes from the table. "And who besides Wiley is hungry?"

A chorus of "I am" exploded as Jack's cell phone, shoved into his back pocket of his jeans, vibrated.

"Darn," the detective mumbled, as he checked the caller readout. "This can't be good."

5

MISSING IN ACTION

FRIDAY EVENING, LABOR DAY WEEKEND

"Hey, Clark," Jack answered briskly.

"Jack, glad I caught you."

An officer and co-worker on the Grosse Ile Police force, Clark Leonard often teamed with Jack and Steve on cases. Clark shared Jack's interest in Michigan's on-going water pollution problems and its effect on fish and wildlife.

"Not calling to cancel are you?" Jack replied jovially to hide his concern something was up workwise. "I'm counting on seeing you and your family tomorrow night."

"That's the plan. We're looking forward to a grand time."

"What's up?" Jack asked. The strain in Clark's voice confirmed there was a darker reason for the call.

Putting him on speakerphone, Jack crossed the kitchen and laid the device on the counter. While he listened, he pulled ingredients for dinner from the refrigerator and placed them on the counter. When he had everything he needed, he closed the door and arranged things by recipe. Next, he turned on the oven. Before him was a huge, glass mixing bowl covered with a damp dish towel. Taking a quick peek, he found his highly desired, homemade biscuit dough had risen nicely and was ready to be rolled, cut into shape, and baked.

"I just got a call," Clark said, "from the National Oceanic and Atmospheric Administration office in Ann Arbor. David Stryker was on Grosse Ile yesterday collecting data."

"We saw him," Jack said. "He was at the West River Marina. Steve talked with him in the parking lot. David's coming tomorrow night too. What about him?"

"He's missing."

"What do you mean, missing?"

If the words didn't do it, Jack's tone killed the peripheral conversation, putting everyone on edge.

"Clark, are you sure?" Jack grumbled. "It must be a holiday! You can always count on trouble."

"Yes, I'm sure. David didn't show for an appointment at the NOAA office last night. He was supposed to meet Tom Monahan, his mentor, around seven and the two were to have dinner. David set the appointment to go over his recent data regarding his doctoral research. When he didn't materialize, Tom let it go, thinking something must have come up or he simply forgot. But today David failed to show to teach either of his classes at U of M."

"Reliability is David's middle name." Worry raised the hairs on Jack's arms. "David's kind of an exceptional guy. A visionary. Have you met him?"

"I have, and heard him speak on several occasions," Clark said. "His clean marina project is good stuff."

"He gave the spiel to the crew team, but those boats hardly cause much recreational pollution. What can I do to help?"

"I'm tracking his yesterday. What time did you see him?"

"I want to say it was around 3:30 p.m. Hold on a minute. Steve's here now. When did we see David yesterday?"

"Hey, Clark," Steve said loudly to be heard. "Jack's right. It was just before four. How close a time do you need?"

"The more precise the better."

Jack quit what he was doing, picked up his phone, and carried it back to the table. As he came towards them, Linn and Bridget got out of their chairs to take over the dinner preparations.

Jack tore off the top sheets from a pad of paper filled with notes about the party. On a clean piece he wrote: *David – no show Thurs. nite.*

Hoping to eavesdrop and not be asked to leave, Wiley slunk down in his seat. He really liked David, who believed great change could be brought about through small means. They'd had some pretty intriguing conversations.

"Some people are deeply destructive to our world," David had told him once, as they talked about the environment. "Thankfully, there are those at the opposite end of the spectrum whose passionate caring makes them activists for good. My interest is for those falling in the middle. This group, when educated about a cause that needs to be addressed are usually willing to help, but may not know how. I want my work to push them gently toward doing the right thing."

Wiley had been lucky enough over the summer to help David outfit storm drains on the Island with plaques warning NO DUMPING - DRAINS TO STREAMS. Runoff water, or 'urban drool' as his father called it, was not filtered or cleaned. Whatever found its way in it (detergent, motor oil, chemicals, and animal feces) ended up in streams that fed into rivers, which poured into the lakes. And lakes were where municipalities drew their water for human consumption.

"Beyond the fact not all water gets treated before it's consumed," David had told Wiley, "the purification processes used today aren't a cure-all no matter how hard we try. Common agents are routinely removed. The real problem is: What doesn't get identified, doesn't get addressed. People dump all sorts of things like medications down the sink or in the toilet that never get identified. The trickledown effect is pretty scary to me."

What was scary to Wiley was previously he'd never given any thought to what came out of the tap. Once he understood he could be drinking fertilizer, or worse, he quickly turned advocate and wholeheartedly backed David's cause to educate the clueless.

"Clark, is there any evidence of foul play?" Steve asked.

"Not that I've heard. The news just came in that he was here checking his pet projects. Someone at the marina saw you talking with him."

Behind him, Steve vaguely heard the refrigerator door open and close.

At six-three, Steve was fit and trim with broad shoulders and long legs. He was taller than Jack and a year older, having just turned forty.

"David," Steve said, trying to remember, "pulled into the marina parking lot in that beat up, old Jeep of his the same time we did. Jack went to talk to the manager and David came over to me. He'd caught sight of my completely stylish, bright yellow hazmat suit in the back seat of the car and asked about it. Our newest nightmare—floating meth labs got his attention. He'd never encountered anyone cooking meth on a boat before."

"Meth scares the hell out of me," Jack said, frankly. "Trying to stop its production is like trying to dry a swamp." His mouth was beginning to water as the smell of baking biscuits permeated the room. He gave his head a good shake and concentrated harder on the conversation.

"As an undergrad, David worked with the Michigan State Police cleaning up drug sites," Steve said. "That's why he recognized the bio suit. I forgot to tell you, Jack, he offered to take water samples if we ever suspect paraphernalia has been dumped. He reiterated what we already know; any boats we find *have* to be destroyed because of the carcinogens."

"Tell me," Clark injected, "Did he mention what he planned to do with the rest of the afternoon?"

"Not really," Steve said. "He started in on a new idea of his to create a nonprofit water farm where purity of the product could be guaranteed. His family owns a huge chunk of undeveloped land in the middle of the state where he wants to build reservoirs."

The biscuits were now a distraction for Steve as well. He lost his train of thought for a second as he glanced longingly at the stove. "I got the impression he was almost finished for the day. Let me think. He said this was his last stop and he wouldn't be long. He wanted to beat the worst of the rush hour traffic on I-94."

"Can't blame him there," Clark said. "I hate that stretch near the airport any time of day."

"I don't have anything more to add," Jack said. "Steve?"

"Nope."

"Okay, call us if you need our help," Jack said.

"Will do," Clark replied.

"It was good you offered our help," Steve told Jack when the call was ended. After inhaling deeply, he added, "But selfishly, if he does, I hope it can wait until after we eat."

"Me, too!" Jack laughed.

SAGE & CHEDDAR POTATO GRATIN

Prep Time: 30 mins • Cook Time: 1 hour

INGREDIENTS

- 2 tsp. **McCormick® Rubbed Sage**
- 1½ tsp. salt
- ½ tsp. **McCormick® Ground Black Pepper**
- 3 pounds Yukon Gold potatoes, peeled and thinly sliced
- 1 large onion, thinly sliced
- 1 package (8 ounces) shredded cheddar cheese (2 cups)
- 1 cup heavy cream
- 1 cup chicken broth

DIRECTIONS

PREHEAT oven to 400°F. Mix sage, salt and pepper in small bowl. Layer ⅓ of the potatoes and ½ of the onion in lightly greased 13 x 9-inch baking dish. Sprinkle with 1 teaspoon of the sage mixture and ⅓ of the cheese. Repeat layers. Top with remaining potatoes, sage mixture and cheese.

STIR broth and cream in medium bowl with wire whisk until well blended. Pour evenly over potatoes.

BAKE 1 hour or until potatoes are tender and top is golden. Let stand 5 minutes before serving.

Serves: Makes 12 servings.

Live Deliciously™

6

POLISHING OFF THE DAY

FRIDAY NIGHT, LABOR DAY WEEKEND

After dinner, Wiley hauled a pail filled with cleaning supplies down to the dock with the intention of sprucing up his boat. In an attempt to be a responsible owner of what to him was a dream machine, he'd made an effort to keep it looking sharp. This pride in taking care of something did not extend to his room, which was often knee-deep in dirty clothes.

Before long, Brian came riding down the side of the lawn on his bike. "Hey, what are you doing?" he called.

Brian had gotten a haircut since crew practice and was sporting, what Jack Davis would call whitewalls, those twin patches of new exposed, shockingly white skin around the ears. Although it looked funny now, Wiley knew they'd be tan by Tuesday, and the cut had been a wise move. Brian looked good. Unconsciously, Wiley ran a hand over his unruly mop. Doing something about his hair had never occurred to him. It was too late now and he didn't see how he could fit it in tomorrow.

"I'm just messing around," Wiley said, "and trying to decide on a movie. Want to stay and watch?"

Brian was still sitting on his bike at the edge of the shoreline. "Sure. I thought you might be playing a game on the computer." He pulled a rolled up comic book from the back pocket of his shorts. "Look what I got. Check out the drawings. They're amazing!"

"Hand it over," Wiley grinned, anxious to see what had captured Brian's attention. Wiley caught the well-aimed throw with one hand. Brian loved to draw anything and everything, but his favorite subject was the future. Wiley had several of his sketches taped to the walls of his room. Taking several minutes to rifle though the pages, he examined the picture on page eleven longer than most. "Flying cars. They're not very aerodynamic, but I'll take this one!"

"I knew it!" Brian laughed. "I want the one on the next page."

After discussing the merits of each, they switched topics.

"Have you decided on what you're going to watch?" Brian asked.

"Either, *Ferris Bueller's Day Off* or…"

"*Bueller? …Bueller? …Bueller?*" Brian cut him off.

"*Where's your brain?*" Wiley shouted back. They both cracked up.

"What a coincidence," Brian said, still chuckling. "I bet besides the fact it's about skipping school, you want to watch *Bueller* because there's a Cameron in the story."

Wiley flinched. Yesterday, this would have been fun to joke about but now it put him on edge. Was Brian going to start bashing him again about Stevie? "Yes, but in the movie, Cameron is a guy."

"Too true!" Brian made a beating motion with his hands. "Drum roll, please. And your second choice?"

"One of the X-Men series, or a Superman? Any work for you?"

"*Bueller? …Bueller?*"

"Yeah," Wiley laughed again. "I'm leaning that way too."

The movie was a success. They hooted and cheered for the teenagers, ate tons of ice cream, and somewhere in the middle Brian got a text from Libby. She was psyched for their adventure. Wiley wished Cameron would get in touch with him, but she didn't, and he knew better than to bug her. Too much, too soon, could ruin everything.

Brian went home around 10:30. "See you tomorrow."

"Thanks for coming over."

7

THE BOY'S TOY

SATURDAY MORNING, LABOR DAY WEEKEND

Anticipation woke Wiley long before his alarm. There was no way he was going to sleep until noon, even if it was the weekend. Lying in bed, his eyes sought his window and the world outside. He praised whatever sun god there might be, for blue was all he saw. Energy coursed through him as he threw off the covers, grabbed his phone from the dresser, and checked the weather—just to be sure. Sunny all day with temperatures reaching the low eighties. Perfect!

He'd gotten up early and had plenty of time, so in the bathroom he examined his face in the mirror. His skin was clear of pimples, as well as any signs of facial hair. Relieved to not have to deal with either of those things, he hopped in and out of the shower in a hurry.

This was a triple deluxe day. He was going out with his friends, he'd be on Sugar Island, and tonight was the party at his house. The only thing missing was the chance to water ski. But both Steve and his dad had promised, weather permitting, if there were no problems from you know who at the party, they'd take everyone Sunday *and* Monday to ski to their hearts' content.

When Wiley got to the kitchen, a most excellent breakfast of French toast and bacon was being kept warm for him in the oven.

It was just the two of them. His father was seated in his usual spot at the table, reading a variety of news sites on his iPad.

Wiley took the plate from the oven, put it on the counter, and slathered the pile of French toast with butter. After drowning it with Michigan maple syrup, he crossed to the table.

"Wow, Dad, this looks really good. Thanks!"

"You're welcome."

"Have you heard anything more about David?"

"I just talked with Clark. There's no news. I offered our help again."

"That's good." Wiley shoved the first of his four strips of bacon in his mouth and picked up his fork. "I just can't believe someone can go missing."

"I know. Listen, Wiley…"

Wiley's forkful of food paused midair. Suddenly, he was filled with suspicion. Was this unexpected breakfast a peace offering for what was coming?

"…this thing with David," his father said. "He was last seen here on Grosse Ile, near the water. It's probably best you cancel your plans to go out and find something else fun to do."

"Dad," Wiley replied in a tight voice, "everyone's practically on their way. Whatever happened to David has nothing to do with us. I know you don't like to talk about the subject with me, but it's been three months of peace and quiet without the zombie showing up. The current probably swept the body out to the middle of the lake where it'll *never* be discovered! You've been out in your boat. My trip is no different."

It nearly killed Wiley to wait and see if this line of reasoning would sway his father's thinking. What he really wanted to explain, and didn't dare, was why today was so important and how hard he'd worked to get Cameron to say yes.

When there was no immediate answer, Wiley added, "We've already agreed to do everything you advised, even doing an E.coli check. There's no harmful buildup of bacteria anywhere near where we're going. I promise to leave my phone on and stay in touch. Please don't worry. We're not going far. You could be there in minutes. We'll be fine."

Sitting impassively, Wiley waited for the final decision. In the past, his dad would never have relented, but he was far more reasonable these days. The fact that he was taking time to even reconsider was a good sign.

"Okay, but check in often and be back by 2 p.m. instead of 3 p.m. That's plenty of time."

Showering his father with thanks, Wiley rose quickly, threw his dish in the dishwasher, and nearly ran out the door before his dad could change his mind.

"Just in time," Wiley yelled, catching sight of Brian. He was leaving the garage, pushing a shiny, red wheelbarrow that held an overstuffed bag and a medium sized cooler.

"*Bueller? ...Bueller?*" Brian was carrying a bag in each hand and grinning like a fool.

"Pile your stuff on and let's get going."

Brian off-loaded his load with a sigh. "My mom got carried away as usual." He quickly mopped the sweat from his forehead.

"Anything good to eat?" Wiley asked. He'd brought mostly drinks.

"Lots of junk. Plus sun stuff and other weird things she insisted we'll need. Is this everything?"

"Yup."

Wiley waited until they were almost at the dock to mention David Stryker's disappearance.

"Wow! What do you think happened to him?"

"I can't imagine," Wiley replied. Then, as though reading Brian's mind he laughed. "No way. David's vanishing act has nothing to do with the zombie."

"I guess," Brian said sheepishly, a bit embarrassed that the thought had actually crossed his mind.

Because of the low level of the river, these days being down by the water's edge wasn't always so great. Sometimes the exposed shoreline smelled like rotting fish. But this morning it wasn't bad. By the time the girls arrived together, Wiley and Brian had their belongings stored underneath the Whaler's front bench seat.

"Hi guys!" Libby called. She sounded happy.

The boys scurried onto the dock to meet and greet. They knew Libby was in a good mood from her voice, but they couldn't see much of her face. It was mostly hidden by a huge, floppy hat that completely covered her strawberry-blonde hair. She wore a blue sundress sprinkled with yellow flowers over her bathing suit and on her feet were blue flip flops. She walked straight by them and onto the boat as though she'd done it a million times.

Cameron, covered in sunscreen, smelled like summer itself. She was dressed in a bright green tank with white shorts. Carrying a heavy tote of her own, her long, chestnut colored hair swished from side to side with each laborious step. As soon as she could, she handed her bag to Wiley, who nearly dropped it.

"What's in here?" he laughed. "This weighs a ton!"

"Some extra clothes, towels, and music. Your boat looks great," she said, looking around. "It's so clean, it gleams. I'm really glad I could make it. Do we have everything?"

"We're good to go," Wiley said, pleased that Cameron seemed okay with his far-from-fancy craft. He followed her on board and set her bag on the floor. There were only two places to sit and Libby was already settled at the bow. Wiley quickly slid behind the stainless steel steering wheel and patted the vacant end of his seat. Cameron joined him.

"Before we shove off," he told the girls quietly, "I need to tell you something." The interior layout of the Whaler was tight and small. With only a bench seat at the bow and one in the middle, they were practically sitting on top of each other. The intimate arrangement made it easy to talk. "I already told Brian. Last night my dad found out David Stryker has gone missing. He was last seen on Grosse Ile the day before yesterday."

"How scary," Libby said softly, her eyes wide with concern.

"Yes, very," Wiley agreed. "But I can't see why it makes a difference to us. My dad almost made me cancel today. I talked him into letting us go to the far side of Sugar, but we have to be back by 2 p.m. Does that still sound okay?"

"I feel bad for David," Brian said. As the official boat launcher, he was standing on the dock waiting to throw in the last line. "It's not like we could be of much help to him. What do you say, Lib?"

"I vote yes, let's go."

"Cameron?" Wiley asked.

"I guess so," she said, slowly. "What a shocker. You worked with David all summer."

"It makes me kind of sick," Wiley confessed, "but trust me, my dad will let us know if there's any news. Then we're in agreement this still sounds fun?"

Everyone nodded yes.

The motor began to purr the minute Wiley turned the key. That sound was Brian's signal to set them free. Throwing the line onto the boat floor, he pushed them from the dock with his foot and nimbly stepped aboard. He quickly settled in the front next to Libby.

"I have an idea," Libby said, peeking out from under her hat and smiling at everyone. "Let's try and find a spot where the beach is fairly free of mussel shells."

"What? You don't like shredded feet?" Brian teased.

"I don't," she said with some sass. "Can't somebody please find a way to get rid of them before they completely take over?"

"What creeps me out is Hydrilla," Cameron said, "and the way it hides underwater and wraps around your legs in surprise. Ugh! I got caught in it once and all I could think of was water snakes."

Wiley laughed as he slowly turned them away from the dock toward open water. As soon as they cleared the no wake zone, he increased the speed making them all grin madly. The warm sun on their bodies was glorious, especially knowing soon they'd be locked up in school and would rarely see the light of day.

To get to their destination they headed slightly southeast, passing around the southern tip of Sugar on their left with the expansive entrance to Lake Erie on their right. Reaching the other side, Wiley was tempted to skip the beach for the Cross Dike and deeper water right behind them. His father might never know and it would be something different. They'd been to Sugar on their own tons of time.

The Cross Dike was a man-made cove created from excess limestone excavated in 1907 to deepen the shallow Detroit River. It made great economic sense to dredge the already heavily trafficked area, because shipping products by water was far easier than by land. Much more money could be made if deep-draft vessels, carrying bigger and heavier loads, could navigate the river as well.

Even when all parties were in agreement, it wasn't easy to get the project up and running. The proposed channel would run in and out of both U.S. and Canadian waters which required a treaty between nations to be drawn. It was signed by the President of the United States *and* His Majesty the King of the United Kingdom of Great Britain and Ireland and of the British Dominions beyond the Seas, and Emperor of India.

Physical work on the Livingstone Channel, named after the design engineer who lived on Grosse Ile, began in 1908. To prevent erosion made by the great rise and fall of displaced water from heavily loaded freighters, much of the excavated limestone was used to build a retaining wall stretching for nearly seven miles. The much beloved Cross Dike was part of the wall.

The Livingstone Channel was a huge financial success. In 1912 alone, 26,465 vessels used the waterway during the 242 days of the year it wasn't frozen. That was three times more ships than passed through the Suez Canal, which experienced no winter and was open all year.

In the end, Wiley decided the risk of breaking his word to his father wasn't worth it. He'd probably never be allowed out again if he got caught, so he cut the motor to a crawl and puttered north as close to the shoreline as possible while looking for a clean stretch of beach.

Brian, restless from sitting, took advantage of their slowed speed and stood up. Taking a well-aimed, playful swipe at the sunhat perched provocatively on Libby's head, he laughed when she ducked in time to make the save. He then swung round and made a face at Wiley and Cameron, before swinging back to lunge again at Libby's head.

"Stop it," she laughed, batting his arm away.

"Hey you two, is this okay?" Wiley asked.

Brian gave the beach a glance. "Looks great."

After grabbing the anchor he waited while Wiley turned the boat toward land. As soon as the bottom began to drag in the sand, Brian stepped up on the side and jumped into shin-deep water. Keeping a tight hold on the anchor line, he waded ashore, buried the anchor in the sand, and waded back for the cooler. In minutes, they'd unloaded everything and set up their stuff on the beach. Libby and Brian went right for the water.

"How cold is it?" Cameron called. Libby was in to her waist.

"It's not," she returned, looking back to shore.

"It's amazing!" Brian yelled over his shoulder. Taking three giant leaps, he dove in, splashing Libby liberally and causing her to shriek.

"You going in?" Wiley asked Cameron.

"Not yet."

He watched as she took a huge beach towel from her bag and spread it out. Then, she rolled a much smaller one into a pillow before laying on her back and closing her eyes.

"I want to get really hot first."

"I think you're already there," Wiley teased.

Cameron grabbed the little towel from behind her head and threw it.

Wiley caught it and, grinning happily, threw it back. Next, he unwrapped his camping chair, a clever combination of straps and cushions that sat right on the ground. With his legs stretched out before him, he leaned back to watch his friends play in the water.

Brian and Libby were making a ton of noise splashing each other. The sky was cloudless, it was not too hot and, to Wiley, it was heaven.

Cameron shrieked when the first drop of water hit her stomach. Fresh out of the lake, Brian was leaning over her blocking her sunshine with his shadow. Grabbing a handful of sand, she threw it at him.

"Come on! Why'd you have to do that, Cameron? Now, I have to get wet again!" Emitting a wild laugh, he ran crazily back into the water.

"Yes, go! You deserve it after dripping on me, you clown," Cameron shouted after him.

Pulling himself out of his chair, Wiley went to the cooler to get a drink. "Anyone want anything?"

Libby was out of the water and drying off with her towel. "Water, please."

"Cameron?" Wiley asked.

"Nothing yet, thanks."

Eventually, Brian joined them. Instead of using his own towel, he playfully pushed Libby aside and laid down on his stomach on hers.

Suddenly, Wiley was up and moving toward the woods. "Did you hear something?" he yelled back.

"Wait, I'm coming with you!" Brian grabbed his flip flops and carried them until he was out of the deep sand. Throwing them down, he slid them on, and hustled after a shoeless Wiley.

A loud groan made the two boys pause at the edge of the tree line. To their amazement, David Stryker walked unsteadily out of the dark right toward them. His shoulders were hunched and he was holding his head with his left hand.

"David," Wiley called, and ran the short distance between them.

"Wiley?" David stopped walking. "Where am I?"

"On the far side of Sugar. How did you get here? Are you hurt?"

"My head is killing me. I think I got clobbered. Feel this! There's a huge knot the size of a walnut on the back of my head."

Wiley and Brian helped him to their spot on the beach. Grabbing his phone, Wiley called his dad.

"Everything okay?" Jack's cool, calm voice was clear as a bell.

"No!" Wiley exclaimed. Afraid he was sending too strong a message he calmed his voice. "We found David. He's been hit on the head and dumped in the woods on Sugar."

"Stay there. Steve and I are leaving now. Does David need medical attention?"

"I don't think so. He can talk okay and he's sitting in a chair drinking a Coke."

"Okay. Give us ten to fifteen minutes."

They heard the rumble of *The Best Spot* before they saw it. Jack pulled in next to Wiley's Whaler.

"David," Steve called, throwing in the anchor. He and Jack slipped easily over the side and waded ashore. "I'm so glad to see you!"

"And me you!" David smiled weakly in return. "I understand I've been missing. These kids have provided a great reception. Actually, their being here saved me."

"What happened? Jack plopped in the sand next to David, who was sitting in Wiley's chair. He didn't want to tower over the man or have him keep looking up. "What do you remember?"

"Not much. I was on the long dock at the marina. A cabin cruiser was tied at the end, where my last line was thrown in the water. I would never have noticed the boat, but the closer I got to it, the more I was convinced I smelled meth fumes."

"You found a floating meth lab blatantly docked at the marina?" Jack asked.

"I think so. Scary, huh?" David took a last sip from his can, turned it upside down, and let a few drops fall to the sand. "Steve, throw me another Coke, will you? It's worked miracles."

Wiley smiled to himself. He was still amazed the soft drink his father hated could offer medicinal benefits.

"Sure." Steve replied. "Anything else? Something to eat?"

"No, thanks."

The cooler lid creaked loudly each time it opened and closed. Steve walked David's request to him and then sat down next to Jack. The day was getting hot, making them all perspire.

"I tried to peek in the window," David continued, after opening the can. "There were curtains, but they weren't closed completely. I remember bending forward with my forehead almost touching the glass. Nothing after that. When I came to, I was really dizzy. I closed my eyes for several minutes and didn't try to move. When I opened them again it was dark. At first I thought it was night, but I quickly realized I was surrounded by trees and a canopy of leaves covered most of the sky. I finally managed to stand, but the dizziness hit me hard and I threw up. Thankfully, it's gone and I feel more like myself."

"Better you were tossed in the woods versus the water," Jack commented dryly. "Rip tides could have swept you into the middle of the lake in a hurry."

"Assuming I could have stayed afloat," David said, grimly.

This time they saw the approaching boat before they heard it.

"That's Clark," Jack said. "I called him to let him know you'd been found and were all right." As the Grosse Ile patrol boat came to rest next to *The Best Spot*, Jack and Steve got to their feet.

"David, look at you. You're okay?" Clark smiled a greeting, wading towards them carrying a huge first aid kit. Todd Kelly, a co-worker was with him.

"Yes I'm fine, Clark, thanks for asking. I got wacked pretty hard and went out. When I woke, the world was spinning."

"We'll get you to Urgent Care, to be on the safe side. Can you walk?" Clark asked. Jack and Steve each offered David a hand. Getting out of Wiley's chair was never easy.

"How's the head?" Steve asked when the man was on his feet. He checked David's pupils, but his eyes looked normal.

"I've got a mild headache, no dizziness."

"Good," Clark said. "Let's get you aboard. Todd will take you back while I scour the woods until he returns."

"Thanks for the help, kids," David called. He waved, but didn't turn around.

"Take care!" Wiley said, speaking for all of them.

As soon as the patrol boat backed away Clark headed for the trees.

"Need a hand?" Jack called.

"Nope, I'm good."

"What a relief David's not badly hurt," Jack said to Steve.

The moment felt so weird to Jack. As a detective he should be dying to get to the bottom of David's situation, but all he wanted to do was sit and rejoice in the beautiful day. It occurred to him this might be a sign of burnout. Certainly, it wasn't his normal.

When Jack flopped back down on the towel the teens couldn't believe it.

Allowing his mind to empty of worry, he remember coming right here often as a kid after skipping school. He'd fall in love with the place every time, luxuriating in having the whole day ahead in which to do nothing.

When he eventually sat up he was grinning. "You know, it's a perfect day for a party! What do you say we load up and go back to the house for lunch? I'm sorry to cut your day short, but once it gets out this is where

David was found, the place will be swimming with officers looking for clues and gawkers looking for thrills. It might be easier for you to be elsewhere. You'll be asked to give a statement but it doesn't have to happen here."

Everyone agreed it was a sound move. It didn't take long before both boats were loaded and moving. At the dock, Jack pushed the fully loaded wheelbarrow to the backdoor. As he entered the house, Linn came through the door right behind him. Her arms were strung with bags full of party preparations and she was carrying a dress on a hanger.

"Hey, babe." Jack stopped to give her a quick kiss on the cheek, then moved past her lugging the cooler. He half dropped it in the middle of the kitchen and quickly filled her in about David. "We're going to make lunch and then go through the kids' story of what happened again."

"Good idea," she said, but her eyes were troubled as she scanned Jack's face trying to read his mood.

Steve came in next, followed closely by two men from the rental store who were there to set up the tables, chairs, tents, and the dance floor.

Pleased to be able to leave the setup in Linn's very capable hands, Jack filled the counter with some good—and not so good for you—things to eat. He was slightly appalled by all the junk he found, but because of the holiday he refrained from commenting when he called everyone to come fill a plate. The kids had handled finding David with maturity and skill. He was proud of them and that was a far more valuable message to give today than what he thought about their food choices. After all, they were teenagers.

8

A FAMILY AFFAIR

On reflection, Sander Firth couldn't honestly say, when he'd taken aim on the Davis dock, if he'd meant to kill his daughter, Sylvia Baron, or not. How much had wishes and desires swayed him in his duty that afternoon last May? He simply couldn't tell. It made his stomach roil every time he tried to think it through. Yet he was fairly certain, if there'd been any prior hint or warning of a personal connection for him in the case, he would have bowed out immediately and let another Keeper of the Watch take his place.

He now found himself drowning in a personal drama that had bedeviled him ever since. The never-ending whisperings running through his mind were agonizing. Had he, or had he not, taken a stand that day and challenged the rules he'd sworn to obey?

The image of the two women standing by the water in the bright sunlight was, and would always remain, crystal clear in his memory.

Heidi, in her late sixties, could still turn his head. Large blue-gray eyes, impossible to ignore, sparkled with intelligence and challenge, while her beautifully cut white hair, and artfully applied makeup presented a picture of competence. Nothing about her well groomed demeanor indicated her life had been anything but rich and satisfying.

The other woman present that day, Sylvia Baron...his daughter, had been born to Heidi when she was fourteen after a brief encounter with him. Forced to give the baby away at birth, Heidi had known little about her daughter until recently. Sander had not known she existed.

Sylvia, at fifty-four, looked more like Heidi's sister, especially since they shared the same, gorgeous eyes. Sylvia's style was less well put together than her mother's, but it worked for her. Instead of being striking like Heidi, she was beautiful.

Within minutes of finding his lost love after so many years, Sander met a daughter he didn't know he had. Next Heidi made a confession that left him in agony as to what to do. Should he live up to the code of ethics he'd sworn to abide as a Keeper of the Watch and rid the world of these two? Or follow his heart and desperate desire to let them go?

To find the woman of his dreams—alive and within touching distance—after so many lost and lonely years was a miracle. To hear her tell him she was a traitor—a betrayer of his trust, nearly killed him. Over the years he'd allowed himself to believe in her. Heidi's disclosure left him feeling duped… tricked, but he didn't blame her for his participation in their game of affection. Only himself.

Watcher Law decreed everyone associated with resurrecting the dead must be exterminated. No exceptions. The risk to human existence, if they knew *anything* about reanimating bodies, was too great. With both women dead the Beyer bloodline ended. The darkest secret of all would pass out of existence.

Once before Sander had chosen to not follow the rules and given his cherished lover freedom. It had proven a good bet for many years. Then it had cost the world, and him, plenty of pain. The final reality of what to do about her, no matter how he felt or how painful it might be, had been a no-brainer. Sander simply couldn't afford to chance it. Guilt sparked by memory of the generations of Keepers who'd put in long years of dedication to a sworn oath, compounded by the fact this resurgent nightmare of reanimated beings threatening mankind again was his fault, freed him to fire a shot.

But killing his daughter?

Discovering that day he had a blood relative—a daughter—after years of thinking he was alone, changed everything. The revelation was so big it nearly crushed him.

Still, he fired.

There'd been no way to measure the personal cost of his actions until he'd felt the recoil of the gun. Then he'd run...from the crime scene, other authorities, his memories, and despair.

Finding out the next day his daughter had survived the shooting left him confused. How could he have missed? He was an excellent marksman. But knowing he had not succeeded in eliminating her, as was his duty, made him feel exhilarated! She was alive! And would make a full recovery—at least physically.

He'd wept, and known instantly he would never go after her again. His heart, after years of loneliness and heartbreak demanded another solution. He had an offspring. Family. Knowing Sylvia walked the earth awoke a primal connection so strong nothing else mattered but to try and forge a future with her.

To say it was complicated was a laugh. This was the worst thing he'd ever faced in his decades of chasing evil. Keeping Sylvia in his life would require two separate fights of such intensity he wasn't sure he could pull them off. But he would die trying.

First, he had to convince his colleagues to give her a chance.

Over the years, with no other close relationships to turn to, his co-workers had become a replacement family of sorts. Sander didn't like one of them, was extremely fond of the other two, but he trusted them all. They'd listened and helped him, backing him when he'd asked permission years ago to allow Heidi Beyer to go free. It was the wrong decision. He should have finished her off, but even then, what was clear in theory was, for him, not as simply defined in practice. He felt for this woman who had paid a horrific price for being born a Beyer. Years ago, by pure chance, he'd found her barely alive, after being tortured by those seeking what they thought she knew. Because of who she was she had not given in and her strength to resist such treatment must be worth something, or so he'd thought at the time.

Looking back, he could admit his becoming entwined with her at such a young age, coupled with finding her near death so many years later, emotionally crippled his thinking. He'd gone to bat for her, seeking consensus from his partners to amend their rule and let her go when she'd promised to keep her secrets to herself—*forever*.

Unfortunately, she'd not held up her side of the bargain. Heidi Beyer had sworn to him she was the last of her family who could possibly know the terrifying secret of how to bring the dead back to life.

He'd never known the extent of her knowledge. It hadn't really mattered. What did matter was that she had given her word to never tell what she knew, if she knew anything at all. Now, thirty-some years later, the consequences of his believing and standing up for her were impossibly painful. How could she have done what she did? To him?

Nothing about the pieces of the story were simple. In fact they were incredibly messy. Heidi's lying to protect her child may have also been to protect him too, depending how you looked at it. If the second part was true, her protection was an incredible gift, giving him years of freedom from the sentimental tangle in which he was now bound.

The more he examined the meaning of what he'd learned, he only sank deeper into an emotional quagmire that left him unsure of pretty much everything having to do with these two women. His suffering continued to rub him raw.

In the end, he didn't approach his professional family; they came to him. "Sylvia Baron is alive. Are we to believe you missed?"

"I honestly don't know if it was intentional or not." Then he presented his argument. "This woman means everything to me. I beg you to give her a chance. There is no proof she is privy to the secret. I will keep her in my care, question her, and teach her what I know."

Collectively the answer was no. "We broke our rules for you once before. This is the daughter of the woman who betrayed you. They've been in each other's company. What kind of a fool have you become?"

"I believe in her. I would like my daughter to work with us. Question her for yourselves. She and I are tied by blood. It is tradition to pass our positions to the next generation, if we deem them worthy. I want to train her to replace me. The world is changing quickly and I'm getting old."

This they understood. Only one of them was under fifty. They'd stopped recruiting long ago, believing there was little need for the services they provided. The universe had been safe, at least from zombies, for quite some time no matter what the tabloids said.

"A new trainee is needed," Sander pushed, "and Sylvia is a computer scientist. That is the future. If you don't like what you hear from her, I will respect your opinion and the subsequent outcome, even if you decide against her."

The Keepers of the Watch relented enough to allow the unprecedented. They would grant Sylvia an interview. But there were conditions, lots of conditions, both for her and Sander.

"If we make allowances," they told him, "she must endure a trial period, an apprenticeship, during which we'll scrutinize her every move. If she proves to *not* be of the caliber necessary to be one of us, will you truly accept our decision?"

"I will." But he wondered with sudden understanding about the risk he was taking. If in the end they thought she knew something, would his resignation be enough to satisfy them? Or would they eliminate him as well because now he was associated with her?

"One last thing. Your training must include not just what we do, but why. She must know the history and the suffering of so many previous generations."

"Agreed."

"Then bring her to us."

Shocked to have gotten this far, Sander suddenly faced his second, and much more difficult challenge. Could he convince Sylvia this was a proposal worthy of consideration?

He called.

"You are filth," she hissed over the phone. "I've had time to think and I cannot believe what you did! You killed my mother and shot me. I will never, do you hear me, *never* have anything to do with you! Leave me alone!"

But she did not hang up.

He talked, cajoled, and debated the pros and cons. He begged. Finally, he gave up and ended the call. It took him weeks to find the nerve to try again.

She'd been waiting. Ensnarled as badly as he in this emotional vortex, she wanted—needed—to hear he was hurting as much as she. The gut-wrenching experience of seeing her newly-found birth mother's life snuffed out, within minutes of meeting her biological father, had stripped her of any kind of defensive armor.

Eventually, after multiple conversations, they met. Through the cracks in Sylvia's shattered heart, her father's plea to listen seeped into her being. Their very tenuous family tie held, and Sylvia accepted his olive branch.

"Here's the deal, Father. I can honor the fact you are my parent, and I thank you for the gifts you have given me. You've lived your life according to the doctrine of generations of your family and that I respect. My mother's side of the family has also honored such an existence. I stand cursed somewhere in the middle of two opposing forces. If you and I can forge any trust between us it will be a miracle. Still, I promise to give it my best."

And she did.

But it cost her. At the slightest hint of betrayal from him she would fly into a rage. It was horrible for Sander to endure. Each time it happened he took it, and when they were done thrashing everything out, their connection was stronger.

Sylvia held her own during the grueling interviews. The Watchers came at her again and again, until they had to admit she knew very little Beyer family history. It was possible she was innocent.

"There is no reason for you to believe me," she said repeatedly. "I know of no other way to prove my loyalty than to remind you I came to Michigan to try and help my mother remedy the mess for which she felt responsible. I *chose* to come. I have never been privy to the Beyer knowledge. I am on your side and prepared to give you my sworn oath. What I offer this group is a new form of expertise, along with my loyalty and enthusiasm. I believe I can capture the remaining zombie. If it exists, it must be destroyed."

At least on the last point they concurred. Although the Watchers failed to find any evidence against Sylvia, they remained reluctant to grant her their final stamp of approval. She was a Beyer after all. They held tight to their demand she serve an apprenticeship. For the next twelve months, her every move would be scrutinized. If she could live with that decision, they would release her into the hands of her father for training.

She said yes.

"I was born on the Isle of Man," Sander said, within minutes of hearing the verdict.

"You're an island boy!" she laughed, instantly releasing the pressure of her interviews into the air.

"I am." He smiled in return, feeling a sudden lift in his spirits at her playfulness. "We'll start there. As I told Jack at our first meeting, I'm more of an I-S-L-E, than an I-L-E man. Pack lots of warm clothing for all kinds of weather. We'll be gone at least two weeks."

9

SYLVIA'S HISTORY LESSON

Sander and Sylvia's flight from Detroit to New York's JFK airport took slightly more than two hours and left them with a four-hour layover. They landed at Heathrow the next morning at 6:35, London time. From there, they took a train north to Liverpool. Sylvia had been to the city before, but had not visited the port area which was their last stop before the Isle of Man.

After retrieving their luggage from the baggage carousel, they headed outside to hail a cab. It was early July, yet a cold rain poured from a tin-colored sky.

"Wait a minute, Dad."

Sylvia stopped walking. Unzipping her suitcase partway, she rummaged around inside with one hand and pulled out a cobalt blue, waterproof rain jacket. After slipping it on, she closed her bag and hurried to catch up with her father, who was better prepared for the sloppy weather.

The taxi to the harbor was stifling, the heater on full blast. Sylvia couldn't get her jacket off fast enough. She found the steamed up windows a nuisance. It was nearly impossible to see any of her new surroundings.

Flying to the Isle of Man, situated halfway between Ireland and England, would take approximately twenty minutes. But Sander reasoned a boat ride would wash away the frantic pace of the past twenty-four hours.

The ferry, which would deposit them on the eastern shore of the island, departed on time. As it chugged out into the Irish Sea, ever increasing waves rocked and rolled the ship. On deck, icy spray stung their cheeks making sightseeing intolerable, so they retreated inside to find something hot to drink. The crossing took just under three hours, putting them into Douglas, the capital and largest city, in the late afternoon.

Sander had made reservations at an enchanting B & B, and the hot bath Sylvia enjoyed after being shown to her room melted away the tired ache in her bones.

In the morning, father met daughter downstairs for an early breakfast. The sky had stopped its crying and the damp of yesterday was replaced by a true summer day. They rented a car to make the overland trip to the place of Sander's birth and the beginning of his story.

"Would you like to drive?" Sander asked, dangling the keys in invitation as they threw their bags into the trunk of a blue Ford Focus. He knew she could drive on the left.

Surprised by the offer, Sylvia smiled widely, but shook her head. "No thanks, unless you don't feel up to it. I want to see everything!"

It was a sparkling morning. They took the A1 west to the opposite shore and the town of Peel. During the first few miles they said little, relaxing and becoming acclimated to the new surroundings. As they began to see signs for Peel, Sander broke the silence.

"I have heard the Isle of Man described in a variety of ways. It is a self-governed British Crown Dependency, located in the Irish Sea between the islands of Great Britain and Ireland. These days, it attracts people interested in private space travel. The lack of humans and the sparse terrain make it a perfect location for such endeavors." He paused. "And it is home to fairies."

Sylvia laughed in delight, causing her rather serious father to smile shyly.

"This island is an ancient habitat," Sander continued. "Humans may have roamed here as far back as 8000 or 9000 BC. Evidence of habitation from a long line of conquests includes Neolithic structures and burial grounds covered with Celtic and Norse crosses. It must have been a tough and stark existence back then. In fact, it still is, requiring a stout heart and plenty of grit. I find the 100 miles of coastline, gushing waterfalls, and deep rock pools breathtakingly beautiful. For others, it feels lonely and barren. Our first port of call, unless you would like lunch first, will be Peel Castle."

"Let's do it. I can wait to eat."

"Good."

To get to St. Patrick's Isle, the site of the castle, they drove across a causeway. Brilliant blue painted the whole landscape, as sky and water became one. Sylvia's heart nearly burst with pleasure.

"The Firths can trace their ancestral line back to the 11th century," Sander said. "They were Vikings and helped build this very structure."

"Really?" Sylvia whispered, trying to picture what being a Viking meant. Of course, she'd seen pictures in books of men wearing conical metal hats and holding spears. Did that image ring true for her ancestors? She couldn't put the two ideas together and get family, but she was no expert on the subject.

"Come and see," her father invited with a warm smile, fully comfortable in this setting.

Peel Castle was impressive! Far more than a broken-down pile of rocks, it was made of red sandstone. The rugged building and archways had a pleasing design. They climbed Gatehouse Tower where the view of the neighboring land and sea was breathtaking. To experience the magnificence of this wondrous place would be amazing for any reason, but for Sylvia, it was life changing. This was her personal history. Once she'd been happily oblivious of her Firth bloodline. How dull the old life she'd inhabited looked now, before all this came her way.

"We could spend hours here," Sander said after a few minutes, "but there is more to see. Are you ready to move on, or do you need more time?"

"I'm ready, but I'm getting hungry. I don't usually eat so much, it must be the air."

"We humans are so much more than just our physical bodies. You are burning up fuel faster than normal because the invisible auric fields surrounding your body are vibrating at a higher frequency. That's the desired state of being, but to prevent energy depletion a balanced intake of food becomes important."

They returned to Peel. The town was bigger and more charming than

Sylvia had imagined. They found a small restaurant where the fish entrée was superb. When the check came, Sander laid money on the table. "Next stop: Peel Cemetery."

Sylvia used the facilities before meeting her father at the front door. As she approached him, she was surprised to see he was softly glowing. Was it from the food? She'd not noticed it while they ate. Could others see it? If so, maybe in this part of the world they didn't find it strange because no one was showing any interest. She clearly remembered the extraordinary meeting between them last spring. Her father had suddenly lit up when he'd spoken directly to her, and she'd been engulfed in a warm energy embrace of love. Love was her word, not his. Well, he'd mentioned fairies being a part of this place. Maybe there was more to discover here—like magic— than just her family roots.

They drove back over the causeway and Sander pulled into the cemetery's parking lot. "My grandparents and parents are buried here."

Nothing they'd encountered so far had thrown her, but coming to this place did. Here was the last resting place for people to whom Sylvia was related. Throwing her shoulders back, she took a deep breath and opened the car door. The minute her foot touched the ground she snapped it back inside, as though she'd been burned.

Her father's eyes twinkled with merriment. "Feel something?" he asked. He'd been hoping this would happen. His body had begun tingling when they landed in England.

"A sizzle. It came up through my foot and up my leg. Like a bolt of…"

"Lightning?" he finished for her. "Now that you feel it, you'll want to learn to cultivate such power. Think of your physical body as a controlling device to store, generate, expand, and re-channel it. The point is not to waste it."

Sylvia turned to face him. "I have no idea what you are talking about." But her big, expressive eyes, shining with excitement and intelligence, melted his already soft heart.

For Sander the shared moment was one he would not forget. His daughter had never, nor probably would ever, be more beautiful to him. He watched patiently as she gathered her wits and opened the car door again.

This time she got all the way out, closed the car door, and managed three steps. As though her feet were on fire, she lifted first one and then the other in a bit of a dance.

"What's happening?" she asked, with a giggle. Taking a deep breath, she planted both feet firmly on the earth.

"I believe this area is a node, or a meeting place, where two or more invisible ley lines of energy converge. Think magic power cables that cross the world. Again, most people aren't aware and this is nothing. Wait until…"

Sylvia wasn't listening. Throwing back her head, she laughed with pure joy as she fell to the ground and rolled over and over, as though she were three instead of fifty-four. When she stopped her antics, she rested on her back, arms and legs spread out wide, breathing hard.

"I trust," Sander said, "you are all right."

"Never better!" Sighing heavily, she scrambled to her feet and brushed herself off. "What a rush."

"I've never gotten used to it. My father was completely unaffected. My mother always knew when I was taking on energy—recharging. She said the color of my hair got lighter and brighter."

"How does it work?" Sylvia asked, intrigued.

"I'm not sure. When my body gets depleted, I find myself mysteriously drawn to a power source."

"Like a divining rod pulled to water?"

"Yes!" Sander laughed. "You have no idea how remarkable it is to be with someone who can understand."

"I'm the lucky one. I've experienced something incredible, plus benefited from your explanation. Do you know anything about why you glow? Can you control it? Do you even know when it's happening?"

"I know it happens, but there doesn't seem to be any purpose to it. The level of intensity you've felt here may increase in Scotland," Sander explained. "Did you ever feel anything in Michigan? It's filled with ley lines."

"Michigan? Really? No, this is the first. And it was something!"

"There's lots of magic in the world, running the full spectrum of dark to light. Once it becomes a part of you, there's no going back to life exempt from that dimension."

She nodded, trying to maintain a degree of seriousness. But she couldn't hold it. Her big, wide smile advertised just how she felt. She was so pleased to be a part of this, and all she wanted was more of the same. "What's next?"

He led her to a patch of headstones near the back of the grounds. "Here are my maternal grandfather and grandmother. Beside them are my father's parents. Here is my father. He was considered an expert in many areas," Sander said. "A cryptographer by trade, he was an accomplished mathematician and had a well-developed interest in architecture. If he were alive today he would be fascinated with technology. And here is my mother."

Sylvia stared in wonder. Pooled tears slowly trickled down her cheeks.

"Do you like the name Sylvia?" Sander asked softly, watching her intently.

"What a coincidence, if you believe in such things." Her voice was just a whisper. She was deeply touched. Her great-grandmother, grandmother, and she shared the same first name.

"Although I can absorb energy," Sander told her, "I did not inherit the ability to use it like both of these women."

"Maybe it's a female trait."

"Let's hope for you! I brought you here to see, hear, and feel. For me, the vibrational frequency in this part of the world is different from any other place I've visited. Energy is a funny thing. Some people give it off, others suck it in. Of course, most don't even notice it exists in any other form than when it's harnessed as an external tool, created solely for their convenience like electricity."

Their next stop was the Firth ancestral residence. The house was a simple structure, now owned by another family who obviously cared for it.

"I have always loved this place," Sander told his daughter a bit wistfully. "It was sold when my grandparents died. Well settled in Scotland, my parents had no reason to return."

After deciding they had seen enough and couldn't absorb any more, Sander drove them back to Douglas. They would overnight at the same B & B, before re-crossing the Irish Sea the next morning, although this time by plane.

About ten miles out of Peel, Sylvia started fidgeting in her seat. "What

I felt wasn't just residue of ethereal vibrations from centuries of human in-habitance?"

"It must certainly play a part. I don't know all that comprises what I experience, I just know I do. Now so do you. Tomorrow we will leave here and head north to the Orkneys. I grew up on the island of Mainland and a visit there might explain a lot."

"Thank you, Father, for bringing me here."

"My pleasure, my dear. My pleasure."

• • •

They took five days to drive to the northern tip of Scotland, stopping in Edinburgh and Inverness to experience both city and country. From Thurso, the ferry crossed the Pentland Firth. In passing the island of Hoy, much of what Sylvia longed to see: Scapa Flow, the deep-water British naval base in operation during World War I & II, was hidden.

They came ashore again at Stromness on the island of Mainland. With the Atlantic Ocean on the west and the North Sea on the east, the Orkneys were a windswept lot, desolate, mostly barren of trees. They overnighted in Stromness, and were back on the road early the next morning.

"Skara Brae is a compilation of several archeological sites," Sander explained as he drove. "As I told you, these islands have been inhabited for thousands of years. My parents were called to the western side of Mainland in the early '50s when a huge storm blew away so much topsoil the outline of a village emerged."

"Imagine the excitement of finding such a hidden treasure," Sylvia breathed deeply. She was leaning forward in her seat, swinging her head back and forth between her father and the window to learn all she could about this unknown world.

"Current thinking," he told her, "is that the different sites of Skara Brae—and each is unique—comprise pieces of what once was a community. We'll also visit the Ring of Brodgar and the Stones of Stenness which are Neolithic monuments and big, showy finds. The Stones of Stenness may be the oldest henge site in the British Isles. The unearthed lesser discoveries of Skara Brae, such as the outlines of homes and abundance of artifacts, offer more insight into the lives of the people of this time period than the mysterious stone structures that catch everyone's attention."

Sander hesitated in his telling. His eyes were shining with a deep sense of satisfaction. It was obvious being here made him very happy. As their car rushed over the ancient land, he gestured with his hands at sky and landscape that looked nothing like Michigan. "The place where we are going, where I came to live at the age of two, is headquarters for the Keepers of the Watch."

"Ah."

They reached Skara Brae in late morning without incident. Thin, wispy clouds floated softly above them. A light breeze was blowing and the temperature was 15 degrees Celsius. Sylvia had on a long-sleeved shirt and a sweater, but after they parked she grabbed her jacket. She thought about a hat, but in the end left it behind.

"Where are the trees?" she asked in wonder, as she looked around.

"The Truffula Trees?"

"You know Dr. Seuss?" Sylvia was surprised anew by the many facets of this man.

"Some children's story that," he snorted. "I found it heartbreaking."

Sylvia nodded. She had too.

"Part of why the Keepers of the Watch agreed to break their rules about you," Sander said, "and at least grant an interview is because of your legacy."

"Because I am your daughter."

"Yes. And your great-grandmother and grandmother were Watchers as well."

"What?" Sylvia cried, turning on him in surprise.

"A bit of a shock, yes?" He smiled reassuringly, but he'd enjoyed her reaction. "Our positions are traditionally passed down from one generation to the next. It is your birthright to be considered. Whether or not it's what you want, the committee allowed you the opportunity to be recognized, heard, and evaluated."

Sylvia was speechless.

"You must be reeling," her father observed. "The Beyer/Firth family dynamics create tremendous opposing pressure."

"As well you know."

"Ha. The story is anything but black and white. In fact, it's pretty gray as far as I can see."

Both father and daughter continued to learn a good many things about each other on their trip. Sylvia was impulsive, Sander had a playful side. Upon their return to the U.S., the two bought a house on Grosse Ile on Elba Island. It became their base of operation and from there they addressed their joint mission: to find the last remaining zombie, if it existed, and exterminate it.

If they accomplished the task it would prove two, if not three things: Sylvia could work productively side-by-side with her father, and that she was loyal to the cause. Sander was also hoping it would convince the world and his colleagues his daughter hated the black magic used to create zombies as much as he did. He firmly believed even if she did know the secret to reanimation, she would never use it to create something vile and evil, no matter the gain.

10

CRASHING THE PARTY

SATURDAY, LABOR DAY WEEKEND

Claire was ready and waiting for Foley and Moreno on Océane II's deck by 9:10 a.m.

"Morning," Niles said, when he caught up to her.

"Look," she said, pointing. "Here they come." She checked her watch. It was 9:54 a.m. "Dependable. ETA was ten."

The captain had powered down the freighter's massive engines thirty minutes ago. As the ship slowed, the swells of water lifting and lowering the huge vessel became more apparent.

Foley and Moreno's craft, the *Joyous*, came effortlessly alongside, making the procedure look simple. When the two boats were secured, Foley stood ready. A boom, with a thick hose attached, swung out from the Océane II and over their vessel. Foley caught the end of the hose and pulled it to him. Crossing the deck, he opened a hatch cover on the floor and shoved the end down in it. The mechanical arm was readjusted once or twice until a steady stream of water began to move between boats.

Foley couldn't help but grin. He loved this part of the job. It was such easy money! The more water he and his partner delivered, the more they got paid.

Spending so much time out on the lake was what thrilled Moreno. Usually, from his vantage point at the trawler's controls, all he could see in any direction was the glorious, mysterious substance called water. To him Lake Erie, the second smallest of the Great Lakes, felt as vast as a sea! He had never seen Lake Superior, the largest, or Lake Michigan for that matter. He was, and had stayed, a local boy with no experience of a greater world. Until he'd stolen his first boat, he'd not even known he loved the water. The next time he got more than one vacation day, he was planning to visit the Atlantic Ocean.

Because of Michigan's abundance, Moreno found the shortage of water in places like California and the drought-struck Midwest baffling. Supposedly China was in the same situation, but since he wasn't entirely sure where that country was, he quickly discounted its need. But, with this much water available right here in Lake Erie, what was the problem? How could the little bit he and Foley were stealing ever make a noticeable dent, let alone drain the lake?

"Heads up, Foley," Moreno radioed, his heartbeat quickening in surprise. "Number one and two are on board and about to get in your face."

Taking his eyes off the water transfer for just a second, Foley found Claire staring down at him from the side of the freighter.

"Hello, Foley," Claire called. Distorted by gravity, her facial features looked grotesque as she hung her head over the side of the ship.

"Ms. Barrett."

"I need to talk to you."

Foley's mind whirled with uncertainty. Why was she here in person when she could call, email, or text as usual? He quickly locked the water hose in place, then walked to the side of the trawler. Shoving his shoulders back, he tried to steel himself for whatever was coming.

"Is it hot down there?" Niles asked. He could see sweat glistening on Foley's face.

Foley was more nervous than hot. Niles' downturned face, in tandem with Claire's, doubled the horror show. If that wasn't bad enough, he suddenly realized he could smell their newest, oh-so-cherished catch of the century! What if Claire and Niles got a whiff and demanded to know what was in their second tank? That could totally screw his plans to sell the creature to the highest bidder.

"I hear," Claire said, interrupting his troubling thoughts, "you are increasing your daily harvesting so you can have a day off."

This is why they are here. Immediately, Foley relaxed. Not because the threat of her presence was gone, but because knowing her hidden agenda gave him a leg up. "We could use the rest," he said simply, hoping to avoid having words.

"Check with us next time before you alter the agreed contract conditions," Claire commanded, making it clear independent thinking would not do.

"Sure thing."

"Now," she said, "we want to discuss a new financial proposition. When you and Moreno are finished, come aboard. I'll have the crew lower a ladder."

"Give us about twenty minutes."

After Foley relayed Claire's expectations to his partner, Moreno turned off the boat's power and Foley stowed away the rest of the equipment.

"What now?" Moreno whispered, while they waited for the ladder to be lowered so they could board the freighter.

"No clue."

The two climbed the wobbly apparatus with a mix of care and agility. Once on deck they were taken to a small meeting room near the bridge. A lone window provided a spectacular view of softly rolling, blue water.

"Pretty cool up here." Foley grinned expansively, but his joviality fell flat.

"Sit," Claire barked. "There's water, coffee, or soft drinks if you are thirsty."

Both men requested water.

"You know about the two zombies shot on Grosse Ile last spring?" Claire asked.

Foley and Moreno nodded yes.

"One was never recovered," Claire said. "It could still be out there, and we want you to be on the lookout for it. If you capture it and bring it to us, we will pay a hefty reward. But there's one condition. The creature cannot be seen. No one must know you have it, or of our interest. If there is any refitting necessary to your vessel to accomplish this task we will cover the cost. Do you have any questions?"

Moreno couldn't believe it! Foley had been right, the stinking thing was valuable! No sooner did they capture the creature, than Océane proclaimed they wanted it. The most important thing for Moreno to do now was keep his mouth shut. This was Foley's deal. He was the one who'd wanted to catch the thing in the first place, so it was his call as to how to play the opportunity.

"No questions," Foley said smoothly. Nothing in his demeanor portrayed unnecessary interest or excitement. "It's yours if we find it and can catch it."

"Very good." Claire rose from her chair, and in so doing declared the meeting over.

• • •

After enjoying a beautifully prepared lunch of fresh broiled perch and beet salad, Claire and Niles got ready to leave the vessel to spend the afternoon ashore.

"What exactly do you have in mind?" Niles asked.

"I want to go to Grosse Ile. The Karlsson/Roth house and lab is still sealed tight so we can't visit there. But Foley and Moreno recently paid cash for a $225,000 house. Seeing their new purchase in person might tell us more about who they are and what they might be planning. We pay them handsomely, but really what do we know about them? They've not been working for us long. I'm curious about their cash flow. If they have their fingers in other pies, maybe we should know the flavors."

"Okay. Anything else?"

"Not yet," she grinned, "but I'll keep you informed."

"That would be helpful. Hey, I just got an idea. Since we're in the water business," Niles ventured, sensing his partner was become more conciliatory, "Let's make a splash!"

Claire glared at him, not understanding.

"The submersible!" Being outside had bolstered Nile's mood. He loved the outdoors. "I know it's crazy to bother with it in such shallow water. It's better suited for the ocean, but who knows what we might come across."

"Simply," Claire said, with a knowing look, "because we can."

Niles' wink forced a reluctant chuckle from her.

The sub was a canary yellow Triton 1000 with a clear bubble top that provided a 360 degree view. Billed as a luxury item, its intended market was the casual thrill seeker who might want a variety of diving experiences (reef, wreck, ice, shark, you name it). Claire had been surprised when Niles, a qualified deep water sub pilot, had fallen in love with the lightest and smallest of the Triton offerings and had purchased it as part of Océane's extensive underwater and recovery fleet. Built for two, the ten-and-a-half foot vessel could descend to only 1,000 feet, which in the ocean was nothing. In Lake Erie, where the average depth was 62 feet, it was pure overkill. But even

Claire had to admit maneuvering the joy stick was more fun than shifting and downshifting a Porsche.

Agreeing reluctantly to his request, Claire had the Océane crew get the sub ready for them while Niles made arrangements for a rental car to meet them on Grosse Ile.

On deck, Niles did a pre-departure check. After they climbed in and secured the hatch a crane picked them up and gently swung them over the side and into the lake. As the submersible began its descent, and water rose higher and higher on the sides of the clear top, Claire felt a catch in her throat. She willed herself to stay calm and not give in to, what she would call, the mental weakness of claustrophobia.

When they were fully submerged, a last ripple of unease shuddered through her at the loss of sunlight. Once she'd adjusted to the exchange of a blue world for a greenish-brownish one, Claire opened to the beauty surrounding her. This was a unique experience that few others would, or could, ever share.

"You know what I like about riding in this machine," Niles said, "besides its cool space-age look, is admiring the genius behind making it work. Down here we have a better view of this relatively unexplored landscape than if we were in a car. Everything's been thought of, including headlights for driving in the dark!"

"What I appreciate," Claire replied, "is the stabilizing system that prevents me from getting nauseous, an A/C unit that keeps the air cool and smelling clean, and the consistency of one atmosphere of pressure so I don't get decompression sickness."

"No one likes getting the bends," Niles said soberly. He'd experienced it once and never wanted to again.

"And," Claire added, really not caring in the least, but knowing it would make him laugh, "I like the color."

They had barely gotten started when the first fish swam into view. Then there was another. Big knots of quagga and zebra mussels covered everything. Debris of all kinds was scattered on the floor. Overhead, the water was clear enough to see the underside of a number of boats floating above them, totally unaware of their existence.

The forty-five minute trip went smoothly. Claire quickly put on her sunglasses as she stepped back on land. *This is more like it,* she thought. Still, she took a second to appreciate the world in which they had just traveled. Its water value was making her very, very rich.

Niles had called ahead for permission to use a guest boat slip at the Grosse Ile Yacht Club. He thought it a gamble to dock in the open for all to see. The submersible could cause a sensation and therefore draw attention to them. But convenience won out. After signing in with their membership ID from a reciprocal club they went straight to the parking lot. The rental car he'd ordered was waiting. Océane's success and the money it brought them made life very, very easy.

"What I'd like to do," Claire said, as she got behind the wheel, "is get coffee to go before we check out Foley and Moreno's new digs."

Kate's Café on Macomb caught their eye. Chic and sophisticated on the outside, it was sharply maintained and well-run on the inside. Claire couldn't help being impressed and surprised such a spot existed so far from a major city.

Within minutes they were back on the road, heading north on East River. When they arrived at the former home of the extremely gifted, and now dead scientists Frieda and Ernst Karlsson/Roth, the empty property left them feeling cold.

"What a waste of intellectual talent," Niles commented softly. "I find it hard to believe the professional focus for such gifted people was the dark art of reanimation."

Claire agreed the death of the Karlssons was a tremendous loss of talent. Not because they'd made a poor career choice, but because all they achieved was lost! Their contribution to Océane's success had been major until their brilliant success fell apart. It ended badly for the scientists and Claire, thankful to have escaped their fate, drove quickly away from the depressing place.

"We're looking for Thorofare." She was finding it hard to maintain the incredibly slow twenty-five mile-per-hour speed limit. "According to GPS, the northern half of the road dissects a Wildlife Sanctuary. Foley and Moreno's house is farther down and interestingly, a canal runs behind their property."

They turned onto a dirt road.

"Get this," Claire continued. "The road here is unpaved. The Sanctuary ends at Horsemill, but Thorofare continues. Our hired hands live on the southern, *civilized* stretch where the road is blacktopped."

"This isn't such a bad spot to hide out," Niles replied, as buildings began to appear. "I like the idea of a canal, except if I was up to no good, being next to open water might make me feel less trapped."

"At least they were smart enough to not buy an extravaganza," Claire said as she found the house. "This doesn't draw unnecessary attention and suits their needs without screaming 'I've got money.'"

"Unless you catch sight of that boathouse they have in back!" Niles exclaimed, craned to see. "Turn around and drive by it again. I can't believe it! It's almost bigger than the house. What could possibly be inside?"

"Bingo," Claire chuckled softly, feeling the thrill of discovery trickle down her spine. She'd known there was something dodgy going on with the two men. "The boathouse must be new; it wasn't mentioned in any description of what they purchased. When I swing by again, take some pictures with your phone."

"What are they up to?" Niles murmured, as he lowered his window and clicked away.

"I'm going to pull over up here. Let's go check it out."

Niles yanked his head back in the car. "And risk getting caught snooping? We left them not long ago, they could be in there. A drive-by will do just fine." Niles rolled the window back up. "You were right about seeing the place. What we've learned is informative. We'll return and explore some more when we think it's safer."

Suddenly, he was glad to be back in the U.S.

With a heavy sigh of acceptance, Claire allowed Niles' fear to drive them away. She went south until Thorofare merged with Meridian, and kept going until she came to the light at the Meridian/Macomb crossroad. At the next light—and there were only two on the Island—she went left on Parkway toward East River.

Niles knew instantly exactly where she was going and it killed his enjoyment of their outing. Claire kept wanting to play with fire and it filled Niles with terror. He'd tried repeatedly to control her behavior, but nothing he said changed her mind. Trapped with her in the car, he fought his panic. Clamping his mouth shut, he forced his body to relax and leaned forward as though he hadn't a care in the world. With a flick of his fingers he turned on the radio. Channel surfing proved unproductive. There was nothing worth listening to, so he turned off the noise and sat back to look out the window. On his left was the Detroit River. On the right, house after majestic house slid by in a blur until they reached a stop sign and were forced to turn right. East River veered inland for about twenty yards, then turned south once again. Houses now sat on both sides of the street and those facing the river were monstrous in size.

"Look at all the cars," Claire said, as they crossed over a small, humped bridge onto tiny Hickory Island. "Someone must be having a party."

Navigating the narrow, worn road crowned in the middle was a slow business. Numerous cars were parked haphazardly, lining both shoulders. Like bees buzzing around a hive, people of all ages were strolling toward a small, yellow, white trimmed clapboard house whose yard was all decked out with twinkling lights and balloons.

Claire gasped in surprise.

"What?" Niles demanded, shrewdly appraising his partner.

"Guess who lives there?"

"You think I don't know? Detective Jack Davis and his son, Wiley. How could you have possibly known he was throwing a bash?"

"I didn't." Seeing Niles' expression, Claire burst out laughing. "I swear! Really, I had no idea. I'll go round and park over on the other side of this grassy area. We can sit and watch who comes and goes."

Niles managed to swallow his indignation at being manipulated and placed in such danger. In the three months since zombie creators, Frieda and Ernst Roth, AKA the Karlssons, were discovered on Grosse Ile, Océane Industries remained unknown as the money behind the scientists' enterprise. Why on earth would Claire risk their good fortune with possible exposure? Coming here, to the home of the detective who had led the raid on the Karlssons' lab, was just plain stupid.

After several minutes of people watching, Claire threw open her door and stepped out.

"What are you doing?" Niles demanded, trying again to exert some control.

"What do they call it, on this side of the pond? Crashing the party?" Wedged between the open door and the car's interior, Claire stood up straight and smoothed down her dress with her palms. "There. I'm going to check it out! How do I look?" she asked cheekily, before turning fully around in the cramped space. "Don't worry." She bent down and poked her head back inside the car. "There are so many people milling about, if I stay on the outskirts of the lawn no one will notice me. Want to come? It's cocktail hour," she teased. "Doesn't a drink sound refreshing?"

"You're talking crazy. Of course you'll be noticed."

But like metal drawn to a magnet, he was powerless to withstand her force. Even though he knew it was madness to go anywhere near Jack Davis, Claire's wild scheme held a certain attraction, especially compared to sitting here alone.

11

EVIL INTENT

"Red sun at night, sailor's delight." Moreno quipped, as he raised his glass. "May the forecast be this good Monday, for our day off!"

The setting sun, about to disappear over the horizon, was glowing like a ball of fire turning the sky and the surface of Lake Erie into a spectacular array of pinks, oranges, and hot reds. Seated on the back deck of a forty-foot cabin cruiser, Moreno and Foley laughed uproariously as they enjoyed the effects of a few drinks on this beautiful evening. The boat's gentle swaying on the open water was due as much to the liquid swirling inside them, as to the liquid swirling beneath them.

"Here's to Océane Industries, our new find, and easy, easy money," Foley toasted in answer. "You have to admit hearing Claire ask us to find the zombie, when we already have it was pretty amazing!"

The two men had known of each other for years. Recently, they'd united ventures to try and make enough money to do more than just exist. It had been a good decision.

It was Moreno's idea to steal a boat. Foley, intrigued with its potential, had decided to detail and outfit it as a lab. He figured a rolling venue would greatly reduce the chance of police detection, and not having to ditch their equipment at a minute's notice to run from the law would be a huge cost savings. It worked beautifully and they quickly established a reputation for reliability when they repeatedly delivered as promised.

Moreno, emboldened by their success, absconded with a second and more expensive model. And then another. The beauty on which they were currently floating had been in their possession for less than two weeks. Foley had just finished refitting and refurbishing it, this time for pleasure only.

Foley rubbed his thumb and fingers of his right hand together in the universal sign for money. "Here's to our good fortune!"

"Hurrah for us!" Moreno said, yet he was hardly jubilant. In fact, he sounded positively gloomy.

"Snap out of it, would 'ya? Why are you so afraid of that creature?"

"First: it's a killing machine. Second: it's *not* reliable. It didn't follow orders and that's how it got loose."

"Well, it's not on the loose anymore. Aren't you pleased to have something Claire wants so badly she will pay us a fortune to get her hands on it?"

"Yes, I'm glad she wants it. Let's make the deal tomorrow. The sooner we get rid of it the better." Sick of the subject, Moreno polished off his drink, then rose to get another. "Want a refill?"

Foley held out his empty glass.

While he was up, Moreno cleared the table and refreshed the snack bowls on the table with nuts, chips and clam dip. He was thinking about getting out some cheese when Foley started with more zombie talk.

"I want to know more about a certain, *Syl-v-ia,* who has come to live on Grosse Ile." Foley let the drawn out the syllables of her name hang in the air. "According to news sources, Ms. Baron is the daughter of Heidi Beyer. Heidi, if you remember, died on the Davis dock last May. According to legend, it was Heidi's long dead ancestor, Richard Beyer, who became a disciple of the dark art of reanimation in order to sell them as slaves to save his destitute family.

"Coincidently, Heidi was shot and killed when the last two zombies created by Grosse Ile scientists rose out of the water to attack. Our creature is one of them. They had gone rogue and Sylvia Baron, Heidi's daughter was trying to recapture them. It's all over the internet Sylvia's a computer brainiac. The whole shebang is shrouded in mystery. But I know this much, if

Heidi was killed because she knew something about creating zombies, her daughter must be in on it too!"

Moreno, his mind dulled by alcohol, could barely follow his partner's reasoning. "At least she doesn't stink."

Foley found that really funny. "Miss Computer Scientist will know about microchips. Have you forgotten our score in Detroit?"

Moreno had. They'd met a guy in a bar who needed a lift out of town, actually out of the country. As payment for slipping him out of the U.S. into Canada, he'd given them some kind of high-powered microchip stolen from a company in California.

"I think we should have a little talk with *Syl-v-ia* about what could happen if the chip was implanted in our prize possession. It might jack up the creature's value and then we can demand a bigger payoff from our friend, Claire!"

After handing Foley his refill, Moreno sat down heavily in his chair and closed his eyes. His partner was an idea man. He got that, but what they were into was too deep for him. Feeling sleepy, he put his head down. If only Foley would calm down and forget about zombie this and zombie that. He was so sick of the subject.

Foley was not offended when his partner checked out of the conversation. Instead, he got up and retrieved his laptop from the cabin. He would make good use of the uninterrupted silence to work on a plan of action. He'd hated being poor and was not about to let this opportunity pass him by.

• • •

Terra firma was no longer familiar. Chained to the wall it longed for water, the creature's only solace.

The urge to submerse itself in the soothing liquid that bathed its physical and psychic wounds pressed down more heavily with each passing hour. The protective gel once covering and caressing its body had washed away. The dry air—after months underwater—was cracking, splitting, and peeling its already carcinogen damaged skin like drought ravaged earth.

It had to get back to the water. Back in the water. Before it was too late.

• • •

12

LET THE PARTY BEGIN

SATURDAY NIGHT, LABOR DAY WEEKEND

By five o'clock Jack was fed up with chores and ready to play. Tonight felt like a triumph over the uncertainty and constant vigilance of the last few months. Sander and Sylvia had assured him they, plus the guards, could handle any trouble. As the day melted into twilight and guests started arriving, he relaxed and vowed to enjoy every minute.

Since the house could never accommodate so many guests, the festivities were taking place outside. The backyard faced the road and had been decorated to make an impression. Every tree and bush was strung with white lights, adding extra twinkle to the abundance of fire flies soon to make a flashy appearance. Large clusters of bright orange, red, yellow, and green helium balloons dotted the grounds and waved in welcome as people sauntered by.

Two rectangular tables, staffed by bartenders, sat on one side of the lawn offering a wide variety of drinks. Covered in lemon linen cloths, the tables were artfully decorated with small bouquets of flowers that matched the balloons. Across the yard, two identical tables offered scrumptious, pre-dinner treats. Scattered in-between, eight round tables with seating for twelve beckoned cheerfully. They, too, were draped in yellow and decorated with candles and more bright spots of flowers mixed with lush greenery.

Wiley had already visited the drinks table and was chugging his first Coke of the night. Showered and dressed in a new shirt and shorts, he stood off to the side of the yard.

"Making plans?" Sylvia asked shrewdly, as she stepped before him. She'd seen him eyeing the balloons.

"Ah, no," he grinned, hoping to cover his surprise. She couldn't know, could she, what he'd been thinking? "I'm just waiting for my friends."

"Wiley," Sander called, arriving with his hands full. "How are you?" He passed a highball glass and napkin to Sylvia, then paused to take a sip of his drink.

"I'm fine, thanks."

Sylvia smiled at the boy's polite response. "He's waiting for his friends," she told her father.

As though summoned by magic, Cameron and Libby appeared before them.

"Cameron, hello!" Sylvia said warmly, pleased to see her.

"Hi Sylvia. This is my friend, Libby Scott. Libby, this is Sylvia Baron and her father, Mr. Firth. Sylvia has been teaching me to write code."

"Libby, it's a pleasure to meet you," Sander said, nodding. "Are you interested in computer science?"

"No, I'm kind of searching for my thing," she said quietly. "I'm joining the drama department to see what that's like."

"How brave!" Sylvia told her. "What would life be without creative endeavor? Our existence would have no color."

Libby beamed with pleasure.

"How are you two?" Wiley asked, turning the questioning back on the adults.

"We are well," Sander told him, "and pleased to be here, with or without a zombie on the loose."

"Wow, you actually said zombie!" Wiley blurted. "Lately, everyone shuts up about the subject the minute I come into the room. As though I don't notice."

"Trying to protect you, huh?" Sylvia asked, cocking her head slightly toward her father.

"Yes!" Wiley's eyes opened in wonder. Had Sylvia signaled she sometimes felt the same? Even at her age? Wiley filed that piece of information away to examine later. "Dad and Steve, along with you were so upfront last spring."

"Tell me," Sander asked, frowning, "how does it make you feel when it happens?"

"Crazy. No one's actually lying to me, but they're not sharing anything about the scary stuff. I suspect it has to do with Linn and Bridget." Wiley knew Sander was good at keeping confidences, so he assumed it was safe to talk freely with Sylvia. "The women are a new addition, a *really* great one, but it changes things. Do they think talking about it to me will make me afraid?"

"Are you?" Sylvia asked seriously.

"Of course!" Wiley laughed, delighted with her question. "But bringing it into the open might make it easier."

Sander nodded in agreement. "Fear closes your heart. Action opens it." How he loved to talk to this boy! Always impressed with Wiley's insights, Sander found his strength and resilience in the face of danger refreshing for one so young.

"You're not afraid?" the boy asked the two adults.

"Not currently," Sander said, "but I have been many times. I'm choosing to remain cautious." He had the strongest desire to share with these kids what he knew about the nature of zombies. That they weren't human. They weren't dead, but *undead*. Bodies forced into unnatural beings. But even with Wiley's openness about the subject, a party setting was not the place to explore such a dark subject.

"Do you think it will come here tonight?" Cameron asked shakily.

Sylvia lifted her head sharply, hearing the fear in Cameron's voice. "Let the expert give us his opinion. Father, since generations of your family have spent their entire lives chasing these things, what do you think?"

Cameron's unease confirmed Sander's instinct. The subject of zombies was not a good one for tonight. "I honestly think if it's out there, all the commotion and lights will drive it away. However, if I'm wrong my daughter and I are here. There's no need to worry. We, or the guards, will deal with it."

The young woman visibly relaxed, pleasing Sander he'd hit the mark.

Brian arrived in his big, boisterous way and that put an end to the discussion. After another round of introductions the teens excused themselves and headed toward the grassy park across the street, far away from adult supervision.

Sander and Sylvia stood quietly, finishing their drinks, and admiring the growing crowd. Since they'd been talking the yard had filled with summer color and happy faces.

"Someone you know?" Sander asked, his eyebrows raised in question as Sylvia inhaled sharply.

His daughter laughed unconvincingly, while turning her back on a woman several yards away. "For a second I thought so, but that would be impossible. I was mistaken. Now, are you ready for something to eat?"

"Lead on, my dear. Something being grilled smells wonderful."

● ● ●

"Hello gorgeous, don't I know you?" Jack whispered, sliding his arm around Linn's waist and pulling her close.

Blushing with pleasure, Linn smiled back appreciatively. "Jack, let me introduce you to my dear friend, Bob Freeman. He was in dental school at U of M while I was in med school. This is his fiancé, Nikki Chambers."

"Say, Jack," Bob said. "I heard about David Stryker. He and I have done some educational work with prisoners who have meth history. I encountered his amazing set of skills when the State Police were worried toxic chemicals had seeped into the aquifer near Ypsilanti. David handled the clean-up with efficiency and speed. Is there any news about him?"

"My son, Wiley, and three friends found him this morning on the far side of Sugar Island. He'd been hit over the head and dumped in the trees."

"How horrible. Is he all right?"

"He will be," Jack said. "I'm glad he was found, but we're sorry he can't be with us tonight. He was snooping around a boat he thought smelled of meth chemicals. I'm shocked by it. There hasn't been much production here for quite a while. Have you seen meth mouth in your practice?"

"No, but I see it regularly in the prisons. I volunteer my time but the damage is hard to overcome. Ingesting methamphetamine orally on a regular basis turns teeth grayish-brown and the minute the roots die, the teeth have no anchor, twist, and fall out. Sometimes the hard enamel layer becomes soft, like the rind of an overripe orange," Bob said, frowning.

Jack shook his head, knowingly. He'd seen his share of human damage from drugs.

"From my perspective," Linn said, "the stuff turns ordinary humans into something close to zombies."

"Like we don't have a problem with that already." Draining off his beer, Jack gave his empty glass to a passing waiter. "Can I get anyone another drink?" No one was ready, so Jack excused himself. "I need to check on the dinner arrangements. It was nice to meet you both."

"Do you need some help?" Linn asked.

"No, stay and enjoy your friends." He kissed her softly on her cheek. "I won't be long."

Jack found the caterers busy removing the hors d'oeuvres and replacing them with a picnic extravaganza. Barbequed ribs, salmon, chicken, kielbasa, hot dogs, hamburgers, corn on the cob, pasta with pesto sauce, green and potato salads, deviled eggs, fresh fruit, marinated green beans with cherry tomatoes, and much more would be followed by three varieties of pie, chocolate mousse cake, more fruit, and cookies. And there was strawberry and vanilla ice cream, hot fudge and caramel sauce.

The simple fare was plentiful, and Jack knew it was good. He'd sampled it all.

13

AT THE SCENE

SATURDAY NIGHT, LABOR DAY WEEKEND

The first thing Claire and Niles did after strolling boldly into the party was order a drink from a smartly dressed waiter. Sipping slowly, they stood quietly in the shadows of a huge maple tree scrutinizing the mingling guests.

"Look at that woman shoveling in her food," Claire snickered unkindly.

"Please, Claire, we are not here to judge the locals." Emboldened by the liquor, a relaxed Niles offered his arm to his partner. "Let's keep moving or someone will begin to wonder why we're so standoffish."

The handsome couple left the backyard and meandered around the corner of the house.

"Guards," Claire whispered, spotting two on the dock and five more spaced across the shoreline. "Wouldn't it be something if the zombie made an appearance tonight?" Her body trembled with excitement at the thought of seeing one in the flesh.

"What an understatement! Calm to chaos in thirty seconds or less." Niles tried to sound nonchalant, but it was unnerving to see the actual dock where, because of their involvement with the Karlssons, Océane's stellar reputation could have been destroyed.

Ignoring her partner, Claire stopped to admire the view. "Sugar Island." She breathed the name with satisfaction. "It's so close you could swim to it."

"According to the news it's where David Stryker, the environmentalist who went missing, was found this morning. The place hardly looks sinister, more majestic, but it must have been torturous getting dumped there. I wonder what the story is about him."

"The place really is spectacular," Claire mumbled, becoming a bit emotional for once. "It's so lush. Set against the darkening sky, with the last light of the setting sun bouncing off the waves, it makes me think anything is possible. Imagine living here and seeing this every day."

The pair let the peacefulness settle into their psyches before finishing their circle around the house. They were ready for another drink when they entered the backyard.

Claire lifted her face and pointed with her nose. "Look, there's the son."

"Hey," Niles exclaimed, when Claire's hand jerked and several drops of her drink splashed him.

Claire was stunned! Sylvia Baron was here! Feeling Niles' eyes on her, she tried to deflect his sudden interest in her reaction by drawing attention to what had alarmed her. "I'm guessing from pictures I've seen, the kid is talking to Sylvia Baron, Heidi Beyer's daughter."

"Where?" Bowled over by opportunity to examine so many of the zombie drama players in the flesh, the fact that Niles was being duped skipped right over him. Swiveling his head wildly, he asked, "Do you recognize anyone else?"

Claire took a deep breath and fought to remain calm. *What will Sylvia do if she sees me? Will she remember our pact to never acknowledge our one and only meeting?*

As much for her benefit and his, Claire placed a calming hand on Nile's arm and answered his question. "No. The man with whom she is standing is probably her father."

"No! A real live Keeper of the Watch in the flesh. This is quite a gathering!"

For Niles, seeing Sander Firth in person was like stumbling across Iron Man. He was legendary! A mysterious entity! And here he was chatting nonchalantly at a party. "The infamous father and daughter have returned to the scene," he whispered softly, his bright blue eyes sparkling with amazement, and a hint of amusement. "They've all become friends? Can we get closer?" He nudged Claire forward. "Maybe we can overhear what they're saying."

Claire's anxiety spiked again. Then a miracle happened. A male friend of Wiley's walked up to the group. Within minutes the kids dispersed and Sylvia and her father moved toward the serving tables where the catering staff was clearing away the first course and replacing it with dinner.

"We lost our chance!" Niles groaned, as he watched everyone's back grow smaller. Looking around he realized dinner was starting to be served and his mental clarity returned. "This area will be thick with people any moment. Have we seen enough?"

"Yes!" Claire gently pushed him toward the street while she kept up a stream of chatter. "Thank you for coming with me, Niles. This was far more amusing than I imagined."

But Niles wasn't listening. "Hold on a minute, Claire." Stopping in his tracks, he caught the attention of a passing waiter and snagged another drink. "Look. There's Jack Davis."

Claire's skin prickled with what she hoped wasn't hives, as they watched the detective approach a petite blonde and pull her close. He was introduced to another couple and soon they were all talking rather seriously.

Niles inched them closer.

"I find David Stryker's ideas fascinating," they heard Jack said. "Here's what he's thinking these days. He wants to start a nonprofit farm to conserve and harvest fresh water on a pristine tract of land his family owns mid-state. The idea is in the incubation stage, but right now he's envisioning deep ponds to capture and collect snow and rainwater that will be syphoned into an aquifer under the property. Because no fertilizers or pesticides have been applied to the land for decades, there's little worry of chemical contamination. Other carcinogens will be filtered naturally. When he perfects the model, it can be franchised out all over the world. Quality and integrity will be protected and maintained through certification similar to licensing for an organic farm. There could be different designations depending on how you want to use and market your product. Any fee money collected can be put toward a micro-lending program or other inventive projects. I think it's brilliant."

"Hear that, Claire?" Niles whispered excitedly. "An entrepreneurial wonder! We should hire him!"

"Hire David Stryker. Interesting…but, Niles," she said, pulling on his sleeve. "It's time to leave."

Niles let Claire pull him away. "I'll get on it tomorrow morning! As soon as we're in the car I want you to tell me your impressions," he said as they walked.

"And I want to hear yours! We gained a lot of information," she replied. *And you only know the half of it.* Pressing the key fob to unlock the car doors, Claire sighed heavily. Seeing Sylvia Baron had rattled her. Only now, after escaping unseen could she admit she'd been foolhardy in coming here, let alone showing her face at the party. What would she have done if Sylvia had said hello?

It was late by the time they arrived at the Yacht Club. After parking the rental car, they were relieved to find the submersible exactly as they had left it. Claire once again climbed in reluctantly. Night diving was far worse for her, but they'd made no other arrangements to get back to the Océane II.

In the tightly enclosed space, the execs planned their next moves. Suspended in the dark liquid other-world, Claire was surprised to feel herself relax. The water soothed her anxiety. By the time they were back on board the Océane II, she was her old self, firmly looking forward to tackling the future.

14

PARTY ON

SATURDAY NIGHT, LABOR DAY WEEKEND

After stuffing themselves from the smorgasbord of grilled specialties, salads, several pasta dishes, and other choices, most of the guests drifted around to the river side of the house. No more standing or sitting. It was time to cut loose.

A twenty-by-twenty foot dance floor had been temporarily erected for the occasion and tunes from the last few decades were being spun by a DJ. Hundreds of lines of mini-lights were strung over the area and in the lower branches of magnificent trees surrounding the space. Citronella torches glowed brightly around the perimeter of the yard to keep the bugs away. Scattered over the grass were card tables glowing with candle light and covered in gingham checked cloths of red, orange, yellow and green. Placed at a ninety degree angle to the house was a heavily populated bar and dessert table, filled with selections of every kind to appeal to a wide range of tastes. No one would go hungry tonight.

"This is so perfect," Wiley muttered softly. Here, in the midnight-moonlight hour, the bright reflection of an almost full moon sparkled off the river. He was dancing with Cameron and thinking about the kisses he'd wangled out of her earlier. *Thank you, Dad, for letting me go in the boat today!* Incredibly, his father, looking completely happy and quite capable, was dancing right next to him with Bridget. A year ago this scenario would have been unimaginable.

Around 11:30, Wiley and Brian walked the girls to Libby's parents' car.

"Thanks for coming everyone," Wiley said, as car doors opened and closed. "Cameron, I'll text what time we're going skiing tomorrow."

"Thanks, Wiley. I had a great time."

"Bye, Lib," Brian said.

"Mañana, Brian."

Wiley was a bit disappointed there'd been no time to snag another kiss before the girls left. But Libby's father had been watching, so with a wave goodbye the boys went back to the dance floor.

Stevie Gail found Wiley eating a handful of M & M's while observing Brian dance with Simone White.

"Want to give it a try?" she asked, with a playful grin.

"Sure!" Wiley threw the last of the candy in the grass and wiped his hands on his shorts. He felt a shiver of something go through him as he willingly followed Stevie toward the center of the floor.

The minute Brian saw them together he sent his friend a look. Wiley saw it, but ignored it, and quickly turned his back cutting Brian off.

One dance led to several until a slow number started.

Now what do I do?

When he didn't do anything, Stevie took charge. "I'm thirsty. Let's get a drink."

"Sounds good," Wiley replied smoothly, but he felt stupid. He should have done something besides just stand there. Had Stevie bewitched him? Although dancing had helped him loosen up and be less nervous, obviously it hadn't been a cure-all. His inactions were forcing Stevie to make all the decisions, but responding to her seemed the best he could.

At the drinks table they made their selections, and then Wiley followed her lead again, this time into the trees and away from the light.

"It's cool you came tonight," Wiley said, hesitantly, feeling his way.

"It's been a blast!" Stevie laughed. "I'm going to have to leave soon, but I'm glad I got to talk to you." Then she moved forward, put her arms around Wiley's neck, and kissed him.

Wiley leaned into it without thinking and wrapped his arms around her slender frame. For a minute, he caught her full attention. He could feel her body heat on his chest. Pressing his long, lean body onto hers, he kissed harder and was rewarded when she opened her mouth and slid out the tip of her tongue. Then, just as quickly she pushed him away.

"Thanks again, Wiley. I'd better go. See you soon."

"See you, Stevie."

Wiley watched her walk away, shaken by what had just happened. When he left the cover of the trees, he practically ran into Brian returning from the dock where he'd gone to pee. His friend walked right past him. Their eyes met, but neither spoke. No words were needed. Wiley understood Brian's message loud and clear. The disapproval radiating off him couldn't be missed.

The party wound down about 1:00 a.m. Jack, Linn, Steve, and Bridget finished off the little cleanup not already accomplished by the caterers. Finally, too tired to remain standing, they trouped into the living room and dropped with pleasure on the couch and into chairs to rehash the events of the night.

"Let me thank you again for suggesting we stay over," Steve began. "Not having to drive home is a good thing."

"Not getting a DUI is better," Jack laughed, "especially from a fellow officer. I can honestly admit I had a great time. It was so normal. For once, absolutely no evil was lurking!"

Slouching on the couch with his arm around Linn, he felt a small twinge of guilt wash over him. He'd not checked in at work for the last several hours. And he wasn't going to do it any time soon.

"Everything went off without a hitch. Nice planning, everyone," Bridget added.

Steve gave a mighty yawn, and slouched down farther in a wide, overstuffed chair to the right of the couch. He patted his thighs, and Bridget came and sat on his lap.

"Wouldn't have happened without the joint effort, so kudos to all," Linn said. "It was wonderful to meet so many new people. I've not seen Bob Freeman for years."

"I liked him," Jack said. "I'm glad he was invited. You never know who you'll meet at your own party!"

It was closer to 2:00 a.m. when Wiley and Brian left the kitchen, having raided the leftovers, and came through the living room on their way to bed. They stopped to say goodnight.

"Are we still going skiing tomorrow?" Wiley asked in front of everyone, not wanting his father to squirm out of his commitment.

"Absolutely!" Jack exclaimed magnanimously. He sat up abruptly and turned to face the boys. "Let the fun continue! Everything's a go. Be downstairs and ready to go at 8:00 a.m. Tell the girls and make sure they aren't late."

Wiley rolled his eyes. Brian's mouth opened in surprise. Steve laughed.

From behind Jack's back, Steve mouthed NO WAY. Shaking his head from side to side with great exaggeration, he held up ten fingers and flashed them repeatedly.

"No problem, Dad," Wiley replied straight-faced. Heading for the stairs, he gave a final wave to the group. "Thanks everyone, it was a great party!"

"Yes, thanks," Brian echoed. His huge yawn made everyone laugh.

A chorus of goodnights and sleep tights drifted after them as the two made their way to Wiley's room. Brian had kept his mouth shut about Stevie, but the incident hung awkwardly between them. Dumping their clothes on the floor, the thoroughly exhausted teens tumbled into bed and were out cold as soon as their heads hit the pillows. Wiley didn't move an inch when Parker jumped up and snuggled in for the night.

15

TO THE FUTURE

SUNDAY, LABOR DAY WEEKEND

Foley and Moreno woke with the sunrise. They were still aboard the boat, still seated at the table in the cabin. Neither had gone to bed.

Moreno made coffee.

Foley daydreamed. "You know, I'm beginning to really like the meth business now we've figured it out. I can see us dealing until we're old and gray. Life's most basic form is all about need. You need food, you need clothes, and you need medical attention. Once you get those things taken care of you can ask yourself, "What do I want?" That's where we are, above struggling to stay alive. It's time to have some of what we want. And guess what? I want more money!"

Moreno couldn't help but laugh.

When the coffee was ready, they moved from the cabin to the outside deck. Plunking themselves down in lounge chairs, they took a minute to enjoy the pink and gray morning. Even this early there were boats cruising the river.

They were anchored off the far side of Stony Island, which sat an easy distance off of the middle of Grosse Ile's east side. They could practically touch Canada, right behind them. Stony was aptly named. The stark, rocky terrain was another result of the dredging of the Livingstone Channel. More huge chunks of limestone made up this island that was now protected by the Grosse Ile Land and Nature Conservancy. The Conservancy was part of the Conservation Crescent in the southern part of the Detroit River. Stony was not a people place, but a haven for wild things such as fish, waterfowl, and a lesser loved, but a very important population: snakes. Many of these ecologically important creatures were on the endangered list, including some whoppers like the Fox Snake. It was completely harmless to humans, but because of coloring and size (3 to 5 feet long with dark brown or black splotches and as thick as a man's wrist) it scared people into killing it. Foley had only seen one, here on Stony.

"You know," Moreno said, "buying the property and building the boat-house was smart. But we have to slow the risks...snatching David Stryker because he was snooping around was stupid." He waited to see Foley's reaction. When his partner didn't respond, he added, "We can't waste the boathouse by using it as a jail."

"I know. And you hate the smell. Well, rest easy. It's almost over. There's only one more thing we need to do. *Syl-v-ia* is the key to moving us up several more financial notches. If we act today, I figure in less than two days the boathouse will be free and clear of bodies and you can have it back."

"Good, because I have my eye on something special and I need the space."

"Okay, let's get moving," Foley said. "We have to collect today's water ration anyway. But first let's go home, and over breakfast I'll tell you about an idea I have and see what you think."

After docking, they cleaned the boat, gathered their trash, and went up to the house. Their new residence was hardly luxurious, but it was far nic-er than anything either of them had owned or lived in before. They took showers and met back in the kitchen. Moreno put together a superb meal of bacon, eggs, and hash browns, while Foley made more coffee. They took their food out onto a large screened in porch that ran half the length of the house on the water side. As they ate, Foley outlined his plan. More than once he stopped to rein in his exuberance in order to convince Moreno what he was proposing was a good idea. Slowly, they came to an understanding.

"It's a dog-eat-dog world," Foley said, once they'd agreed. "Or maybe for those of us who live on the water, it's a rat-eat-rat world. In any case, here's to our getting to the top!"

16

GETTING WHAT SHE WANTS

SUNDAY, LABOR DAY WEEKEND

Seated at the table in their two-bedroom suite on the Océane II, Niles was working his way through the Michigan news sites on his iPad. He and Claire had gotten up early and banged out a press release to wow Michiganders with her brilliant new plan. Detroit's bankruptcy was playing right into their hand. The city had to get a handle on spending and get out of debt, or go down in flames.

One of the area's hardest hit municipal services was the water and sewage department. Recent headlines screamed Detroit would soon be raising prices by 18 percent. On top of that, the city had turned off the tap to more than 14,000 delinquent water customers who collectively owed millions.

Océane Industries was going to propose they come to the city's rescue. The company would subsidize the cost of monitoring and cleaning Detroit's water for the next ten years. Claire and Niles felt it highly probable Desperate Detroit would say yes to their helping hand to give the city time to lessen its debt and stabilize its financial situation.

A yes for Océane would give their company their first long-term opening into the workings of a major municipal water system. A ten-year contract would position them in a much more favorable and valuable situation than doing one-time individual contracts, which they were doing now.

Océane would begin their seductive campaign by guaranteeing the city's potable water would have clean color, great taste, and no odor. Once customers were reassured what was being offered would not kill them, and the cost for such satisfaction would be far less per month than what they were currently paying, why would they say no?

"Okay, let's look at David Stryker," Claire said, rubbing her hands together eagerly.

"A water farm," Niles snickered, remembering the overheard conversation. "How amusing. When I googled him, Stryker came up as an Ann Arbor hotshot involved in a wide range of environmental issues."

"What shall we offer him?"

"For starters, how about the chance to work for a renowned water corporation with unlimited funding, while being able to stay in Michigan to finish his Ph.D." Niles was enjoying being fully challenged after months of the same old thing. And to be honest, the experience was made better by Claire's fine analytical skills. *Could I please continue to have this type of future instead of having to endure a bunch of wild schemes, whose danger outweighs their value?* But he told Claire none of this. Instead, he continued exploring what was possible. "As an added incentive, we can fill his head with the idea of covering all his start-up fees, etc. for his entrepreneurial wish list. We believe he is the future…yadda, yadda, yadda. Let me send a quick email to HR and the lawyers. We can contact him today."

Their afternoon was heavily scheduled. They would meet and greet people from the Great Lakes Science Center, a part of the United States Geological Survey, and other local agencies to discuss invasive species threatening the Great Lakes. Océane's newest innovation, a way to clean industrial intake pipes severely clogged with non-native zebra and quagga mussels was being received with praise. People couldn't hear enough about this good news.

Sadly, Océane didn't have much else to offer to reduce the state's 'global swarming' hysteria. Michiganders were already up in arms about the influx of invasive species, but they didn't have any way to effectively go against the enemy. Many of the environmental destroyers appeared invincible. Certainly, they were creepy. For example the northern snakehead, or as it was affectionately called, the Frankenfish, was terrifying for many reasons. Able to breathe air, it could walk on land and stay out of water up to three days. Its row of razor sharp teeth allowed it to eat just about anything.

Then there were the Asian carp. The Bighead truly lived up to its name. A voracious eater, it could grow to 110 pounds, the size of an average 5th grader. One of the most feared, the Silver, had a tendency to jump out of water into boats. At 60 pounds, if it slammed into someone the result wasn't the least bit funny. All these nightmares were swimming their way north, poised to enter Michigan's water systems. They were as welcome as small pox.

"Okay," Niles said, having sent the emails. "What next?"

"We should drive by Foley and Moreno's place again. There's time before our meeting later this afternoon."

"Lunch first?"

"Sure," Claire said, surprised to find she was hungry.

"The more I think about it, I'm convinced there's something weird about the size of their boathouse," Niles said.

"I agree. And your idea to hire David Stryker was a good one. We should own him."

"He'll be an easy conquest." Niles chucked lightly, pleased by the compliment and that Claire was confiding in him again. Their ideas were meshing smoothly, making it feel like old times. "Just like our irresistible proposal to Desperate Detroit, how could Stryker turn us down when we can do what no one else can? We'll offer him whatever he wants! Cash flow is currently *not* a problem for Océane, even without the income expected from your spectacular idea."

17

TAKEN

SUNDAY, LABOR DAY WEEKEND

"It's not as though I didn't eat enough food last night at the party," Sylvia told her father. "Breakfast at Kate's Café just makes me happy." Clicking on her seat belt, she laid her head back on the head rest and patted her stomach.

"It was good," Sander agreed, "I was hungry." He had opted for a less-filling omelet rather than a short stack of pancakes. "Shall we drive around a bit?" he asked, starting the car. "It's a beauty of a morning."

"And it's supposed to get hot this afternoon. Tell me," Sylvia asked out of the blue. "Are monsters a creation of function, or design, or both? Dracula, the Hunchback of Notre Dame, even King Kong—these monsters have at least one physical attribute which enhances the evil they construe. Their physical design advertises an abnormal function."

"What about Cookie Monster?"

"First you know about Dr. Seuss and now Sesame Street?" Sylvia giggled.

"I am well informed! Cookie Monster's physical oddity is he's blue. An interesting design consideration, one that doesn't fit your theory. Blue is a calming color…and it was purposely chosen to portray a monster."

"A *kind* monster," Sylvia replied, cheerfully. "Have you thought about this before?"

"Through my many years in the zombie business," Sander said, "I have wondered why they look the way they do. These ghastly creations were once normal looking people. Why does their appearance change so drastically? Does their physical form reflect *their* evil, or the evil used in creating *them*?"

"What about *The Picture of Dorian Gray?* His outward image remained the same during his descent from purity to moral corruption. It was the painting of him that took on the characteristics of a monster."

"Ha! Oscar Wilde. That was quite a story."

"Don't forget the creators. Were they born monsters themselves?" Sylvia's mind churned with questions. "Or did they evolve into something depraved?"

"I believe both things happen. Some humans are born evil. Others morph downward due to circumstances and life events. Zombies aren't creators, they're manufactured, but do they evolve? Or do they remain 'as is' from the time of conception? I have no idea." A ripple of disgust slid through Sander. "I have a confession."

"Okay."

"As much as I abhor the making of these creatures, the dark side of me would like to see a transfiguration. I've not actually seen many zombies, and never one newly reanimated. On the few occasions I've observed them up close, I've tried to find a spark of individuality in their faces. Usually their emptiness of spirit is so prevalent it masks any uniqueness."

Sylvia thought about this for a minute. "Back to my original question," she mused, "we've determined you don't have to look the part to be a monster. There are plenty of regular looking people wandering around who fit the label purely by their actions."

"A definition of what constitutes a monster might help."

"What about my mother?" Sylvia was surprised to find she had said this out loud. "Would she fit the description?"

"Of a monster?" Sander was taken aback. "Hardly! She never purposely took action against another to harm or gain financially. She just knew a monstrous secret."

"That she did."

"Please don't think badly about your mother, Sylvia. She deserves better. She was used. Caught and trapped in a painful existence of others' making."

"Yes, thank you. I agree. Our talk has given me an idea. We should conduct a study entitled something like, *The Study of Monsters and How They Evolve*. We could examine any number of concepts."

"It's a great idea! I'm not sure where it might get published, but a joint project is very attractive to me. Question #1: Is there a commonality in people who overtake the lives of others for their own will?"

"Maybe secrets?" Sylvia replied immediately. "Their weight can be so heavy."

"And damaging. The longer you carry secrets, the heavier they get."

"Becoming dark shadows in our minds that fester," Sylvia said.

"Fester—good word. Hurtful events, stuffed down inside and hidden away instead of being acknowledged can have devastating results. Those kind of remembrances fester."

"And when the psychic damage goes on for generations...," Sylvia paused.

"It makes individuals or a family look cursed?" Sander finished.

"Exactly." Sylvia shivered. The possibility both she and her father were cursed tormented her. Certainly, monsters had decimated her family. But on this sunny summer day, she didn't want to examine the personal. "Back to zombies. Who's the bigger monster? Zombies who are created and act monstrously, or the creators who instigate evil?"

"Another hard question. The zombie, lacking an ability to think can't defend itself. It's turned into a monster by someone else's design. The human creators are monstrous because of the function they provide...because of what they do. You know how I feel about those who defile dead bodies. To me, they are by far the worst of the two."

"Because the dead have no say."

"Using a person or its body without consent is despicable. Is this conversation getting too gruesome?" Sander turned his head and checked the rearview mirror.

They were on Groh Road, traveling west to east and just passing the Grosse Ile Municipal Airport. It had been a Naval Air Station from 1927 to 1969. Beginning on or around August, 1941, before the United States entered WWII, it was the primary flight training facility for British RAF pilots. Of the 300 cadets arriving each month, many were quickly eliminated. Only those who didn't wash out after thirty days continued on to Pensacola to finish their instruction.

With the devastating damage inflicted on December 7, 1942, to Pearl Harbor, the United States Navy shifted its emphasis away from battleships. There was a bigger, newer, more deadly war innovation: aircraft carriers. The Grosse Ile training station was quickly nicknamed the Unsinkable Aircraft Carrier when it began instructing cadets in a brand new skill set. One vital to maintaining and utilizing a brand-new technology.

Sander turned left when Groh Road dead ended at East River. Ten yards later, he made a quick right onto Elba Island. Their driveway was ahead on the right. Parked on the shoulder of the road just shy of their house was a silver Lexus sedan with its trunk up. A well-dressed man in his middle thirties was standing next to the driver's door. At their approach he waved.

"Will you slow down?" Sylvia asked. "Let's see if we can help."

Sander shook his head. "Call the police and let them deal with it."

"What? Does he look like a monster?" Sylvia joked. "Not everyone is rotten to the core, you know."

Touching the brake softly, Sander drove just past the stranger's car before stopping. He backed up slowly until Sylvia was face to face with the man.

"Hello," she said cheerily out her window. "Is there a problem?"

"Thanks for stopping," the man chuckled. Pulling a handkerchief from his pocket he wiped his face. "It's getting hot, isn't it? I have a flat and my cell phone is out of juice. Would you be able to call AAA for me?"

"Sure, just a minute."

Sylvia grabbed her purse from the floor by her feet and found her phone. While she looked up the number, Sander moved the car and parked in front of the distressed vehicle.

"When you get someone on the line," he said, as he checked the side and rearview mirrors before unbuckling his seatbelt, "don't get out of the car. Give me your phone and I'll hand it through the window."

As though she hadn't heard a thing, with the phone to her ear Sylvia popped her seatbelt and opened the door. Striding confidently toward the stranded man, she presented him with a grin that was a bit extreme, and held out her phone. "Here you go!"

The man smiled in thanks and reached for the device. As soon as his hand closed around it, he threw it away. Then he grabbed both of Sylvia's arms above the elbows.

The next she knew, she was face down on the hot, hard ground with the man's foot pressed squarely into the middle of her back. Fighting for air, she sucked in a big mouthful of dirt that tasted of asphalt. Her frantic squirming did nothing more than grind loose gravel bits into her face, arms, and legs.

Sander had not moved. Still sitting behind the wheel, he was fuming over Sylvia's blatant disregard of his instructions. Closing his eyes, he put his head back on the headrest to let his heart rate settle back down. They had worked on her impulsiveness to jump into a situation without fully under-standing it during their many hours of training. One of these days, he'd told her, that kind of behavior was going to land her in trouble.

After exhaling deeply for the third time, Sander opened his eyes. Unable to locate Sylvia or the man in distress in any of his mirrors, he reached for the door handle. His eye caught a flash of movement in the side mirror. A different man, bent at the waist, was creeping along the side of the car to-wards his door.

Before Sander could push the lock button, the door was flung open. Grabbed by the collar, he was pulled brutally out of his seat to the ground. He landed shoulders first.

Sylvia, still pinned under the other man's foot, could no longer hold her head up to see. She laid her cheek in the dirt and the relief to her aching neck was immediate. At the sound of a car door opening, she whipped her head up again and saw her father pulled from the car, landing hard on the ground. He was kicked twice in the side by a man she'd never seen before.

Almost immediately something heavy thumped down next to her. She recognized the scent of father's soap. After hearing the sharp sound of rip-ping tape, her arms were pulled roughly together behind her back. Her arms and legs were bound, after which she was roughly flipped over. The crush of her awkwardly positioned arms against the ground caused her to cry out.

A heavy hand, pressing down on her mouth, squelched any further sound. Another piece of tape, pulled tightly across her mouth, pinched her skin unmercifully. Solely dependent on her nose to breath, she instinctively blew out hard to clear her nostrils. Snot laced with gravel dust shot out. Before her eyes were sealed shut a bit of luck came her way. She got a good look at the second man's face.

The second her world went dark, panic spread through every inch of her body. Her chest heaved with each noisy and tortured breath she took. Startled by a loud grunt beside her, she held her breath to hear more clearly. A car door opened, the air next to her stirred, a car door slammed.

She let the trapped air from her lungs out in a whoosh. For one joyous moment the excruciating pain in her arms and shoulders eased as she was lifted from the ground like a bag of trash. The relief ended as she was dragged and thrown carelessly into the backseat of the abductor's Lexus. She landed flat on top of her father.

A few strands of her hair were caught when the door was slammed shut. She tore herself free and pressure from built-up tears unable to be shed made her eyes throb. Because she couldn't see, she felt *and* heard the tires squeal underneath her as the car sped off. It hit a pothole so hard she was sent sailing three inches up off the seat. Her father, unpinned beneath her, slid sideways onto the floor. She almost laughed as she crashed back down onto the upholstery. How ridiculous she must look trussed tightly like a stuffed turkey ready for roasting. And she was as good as cooked. Her cheeks, raw beneath the tight tape, flushed hotly with anger and shame. Her egocentric, adolescent behavior, inexcusable in someone her age, was the sole cause of their nasty situation.

Had she really been so stupid as to ignore her parent's advice?

She struggled to tame her wild thoughts and channel her energy. Feeling sorry for herself would not help. She needed options and her list was slim. A voice from the front seat startled her. She'd forgotten about her abductors.

"What do you want to do with him?" Pausing for a minute, the voice spoke again. "Nah, he's just baggage. We'll dump him."

Her father wasn't the target.

"Yeah, good, good." Another pause. "Of course we can make her spill!"

Sylvia's head throbbed with the effort to listen.

"No worries. It's like following a recipe." A sick, raucous laughter filled the car. "You start with a dead body…"

Of course. The Beyer Curse. Whoever was driving thought she knew how to cook up a batch of creatures.

"Oh, that's good!" the man laughed some more. "A Keeper of the Watch turned zombie!"

She dared not cry. A sob might choke her.

A meaner, crueler chuckle made her cringe. "Then we'll have two!"

Sylvia struggled against the tape as ugly images flashed through her mind. Her body ached from being twisted like a pretzel. What was going to happen to her? Saliva poured into her mouth. She swallowed hard. *Think, woman!* Where were they going?

After the car was started it was turned around. They had turned right only once, so they must be heading north on East River.

The car swerved and Sylvia slid over two inches, hanging precariously above her father's inert form. Would she crush him if she fell on top of him? When she got herself back on the seat she raised her rear in the air. Like an inchworm she scooted backwards until she hooked the toes of her flats down between the seat and door. Her toe-hold held as she was pulled toward the floor when they suddenly turned left.

Not having lived on Grosse Ile for long, Sylvia cursed her lack of geographic knowledge. She struggled to picture their route. They hadn't fully stopped for the last turn, meaning the intersection wasn't congested. That could mean Parkway or Belleview. It couldn't be Macomb; the car was currently moving steadily and that would be impossible on the crowded business district street.

She willed herself to lay still and quiet her mind when nausea threatened to overtake her. What would happen if she threw up with her mouth taped shut? Feeling the car slow, she fought to understand. Again, there was a quick stop, but this time they went right onto what must be Meridian. More details came to her. If they paused for an extended time it would mean they were at the Meridian/Parkway stoplight. If they turned left and drove off Grosse Ile the car tires would hum on the metal grid floor of the Free

Bridge. No turn and no hum would signal they were traveling north up the middle of the Island.

The car stopped for what seemed an eternity. How long was a stoplight? Eventually, it moved forward. She tried to picture the Meridian cross streets. When the car veered slightly to the right, it made no sense until she remembered Thorofare. She'd thought the name rather cute when she'd first encountered it. Getting her bearings again, she saw the canal in her mind. Within minutes the car slowed, turned right, and stopped short.

The car's backdoor exploded open. Powerful hands grabbed her legs and pulled her out. Dumped with her face in the grass, the intense smell of weed killer made it hard to breath. The shuffling of feet near her head was frightening. Both men were there, each had a distinct smell. After being hauled roughly to her feet, she was thrown over a shoulder, and lugged 520 steps. Keys jangled, a lock clicked, and a door hinge squeaked loudly. She was carried a few more steps and dropped onto the floor on her side.

Keys jangled, a loud click, and then blessed silence. Sylvia tried to use the 3 remaining senses left to her—sound, smell, and touch—to take inventory of her new surroundings. Dare she trust in the sixth sense of intuition? The more information she could collect, the less she'd have to rely on guessing in the dark.

Water lapped gently near her.

The air felt dank and clammy.

She was probably in a boathouse.

There was a slight smell of gasoline.

Another odor...stronger. Rancid.

Vomit burned up her throat. Sylvia swallowed and swallowed the urge to purge. Memories—triggered by the atrocious smell—of standing with her mother on the Davis dock. They'd been so happy. Newly united mother and daughter were going to end the zombie crisis and make things right.

Next her father, a Keeper of the Watch, sent her mother into the water with a blast from his gun. Her arm burning with fire, then blackness. And now this...what exactly had they done with her father?

She had to get free.

Rolling slightly onto her back she managed to sit up. She scooted several feet until a sliver jabbed into her skin. Leaning to the side, she stretched her shackled arms and felt for the tiny piece of wood. She grasped the tip with shaking fingers. It pulled out easily and instantly the pain was gone.

Something scurried. Fighting the dark thoughts and bizarre images crowding her mind, Sylvia prayed it was mice, not rats. It was neither.

It was something much worse.

18

WHAT YOU SEE...

SUNDAY, LABOR DAY WEEKEND

Claire was surprised and pleased by the scrumptious lunch. The Océane executives left Macomb Street at a leisurely pace, heading north on East River.

Niles rolled down his window and breathed deeply. There was a dryness to the air that made it easy to believe fall was approaching, with winter close behind.

Claire chuckled to herself at her partner's action. It was such a Niles thing to do. She was surprised to be enjoying his company. The adrenaline rush she'd experienced planning a future for their business with him, had felt good. Of course the scope of design she envisioned for Océane would eventually bring them into conflict again, but she didn't have to think about that now. It was far more important not to push Niles out of his comfort zone to obtain the best of his expertise while he remained open and willing.

At Church Road, they left the river behind and drove inland until they reached Thorofare. This time when they passed Foley and Moreno's residence there were two cars in the driveway.

"Slow down, Claire," Niles whispered. "I think that's Moreno in the second car."

"Is Foley in the first?" Claire squinted, and stretched over the steering wheel to get a better look.

"Yes, I think so."

They dared not linger. Claire picked up speed for the next quarter mile and then turned around in a driveway. She drove back slowly. The rear door was wide open on the car closest to the street. Both men were visible and recognizable. They were having an intense discussion, until Moreno leaned over and stuck his head and shoulders inside the car. He pulled out almost immediately, and began gestured wildly with his hands.

"Hold on," Claire said, as they passed the house again. "I'll make this fast."

"Don't worry. They're too engrossed in whatever they're doing to notice us," Niles said, confidently.

"I hope so."

The car door was closed on their return. The men were heading toward the boathouse. Slung over Moreno's shoulder was a body, bobbing face-down against his back.

"Look at the hair!" Claire shouted in surprise at Niles. "That looks like Sylvia Baron!" Having just seen her last night, Claire was pretty sure of her identification. But now what? Niles must never know she knew the woman.

"It could be, even without seeing her face." Niles was talking a mile a minute. "Are her hands bound behind her back? They've kidnapped her? Why in the world would they do that? It *must* have to do with the zombie. They think she knows something!"

Claire slammed on the brakes. Placing her arm on the back of Niles' seat, she twisted her upper torso around as far as possible to look behind her. "Foley and Moreno…those little creeps! Do you think they've found the creature? If they have it and didn't tell us I'll murder them. I asked them for it yesterday."

"Claire," Niles pleaded, "keep going. You can't stop here with the two of them around!"

"You're right." The shock on Niles's face and the truth of his words reemphasized just how dangerous the situation was for them. She gently pressed the gas pedal. "What have we learned? How can we use what we know?"

"It's a kidnapping. There's no other reason for carrying an adult over one's shoulder like a sack of potatoes. We have to call the police. That woman's in danger! We must help her!"

"Wait! Do we just want to screw Foley and Moreno by telling the authorities, or is there a better move?" *Action taken too soon could win us a small victory, but it could cause us to lose what matters most in the long run. If these two have the zombie, how do I get my hands on it? And what kind of allegiance, if any, do I owe the woman who once vowed to help Océane Industries and me?* Claire wondered silently. She took a very deep breath and let it out slowly.

"The woman's life is in danger!" Niles cried. "Our only move is to call the police!"

"Okay, but I don't want to get involved. This needs to be done anonymously. The call must be untraceable, so no cell phone. Let's go find a landline."

19

CLEARING THE CONFUSION

SUNDAY MORNING, LABOR DAY WEEKEND

Jack was the first one downstairs. Relishing the peace and quiet, he poured a mug of java from the coffee machine which had been primed and timed the night before. He let Parker out and grabbed a plastic wrapped, but still slightly soaked, New York Times from the dewy lawn. After feeding the dog, he settled at the table. He had half-an-hour.

Finished with sports news, Jack got up and made his way to the fridge. He rummaged around, finally taking out everything he thought he would need to make a breakfast worthy of a holiday.

"What are you doing?" Linn asked sleepily, padding soundlessly into the room. She was dressed and showered, but still not fully awake. "You're up early." After giving him a quick kiss, she found a mug and poured herself some coffee.

"A bad habit," he replied with a smile, "Hungry?"

"Soon, but first can we talk? This may not be a great time, but there are things I want to run by you before the day takes off."

"Of course. I always want to hear what you have to say. Come with me." Leaving the breakfast ingredients, Jack led Linn to the living room. When they were seated, he said, "How wonderful to be alone." He put his coffee down on the table. "Now tell me straight from the heart, what's bothering you?"

"We share many things in common. You and I work for the good of others. Yet, there is a fundamental difference in our approach to what we do. We come at it from different angles, and I see that as a tricky problem that can ruin our relationship."

Jack's face showed his surprise. This was not what he'd thought she'd want to discuss. Filled with curiosity, he gave her his full attention.

"You thrive in a physically violent world. To be effective, you need to be front and center in whatever is going down—in the heart-stopping drama—where the physical risk is the greatest. You, the man of whom I am becoming quite fond, put yourself on the line to protect others. I understand this and am proud of you for doing it, yet the consequences are rarely benign. There can be trauma.

"Trauma is also part of my life. But as a surgeon, I encounter it after the fact on the operating table. My job is to repair damage. Sometimes it works, sometimes it doesn't. Most people never realize as a healer, heartache and pain are my companions. Therefore, my instinct is to prevent any chance of injury before it can occur. You walk straight into it."

She saw his surprise, but when he kept quiet she finished what she needed to say.

"I think I've been trying to avoid this conversation, but sidestepping won't help things. It seems utterly insane to me to go skiing today. If that horribly destructive thing is out there, it lives in the water! We'd be placing ourselves in its territory, increasing the chance it will harm us. Flirting with danger is not my style."

"Is that how you see this?" Jack asked honestly.

"Yes, and I'm not trying to be irrational. We four adults are highly trained individuals in our respective professions. Why would we risk putting ourselves in danger?"

"Because of our professional value?"

"The personal value comes first, of course. The threat of losing you, or Wiley, or Steve, or Bridget, or the girls makes me nuts. But we have studied, trained, and practiced our skills for decades. The collective loss of good we can do would be wasted."

"Let me see if I have this right. Going skiing today seems irresponsible?"

There was no hint of mockery in Jack's tone, but Linn cringed at his words. "It does to me."

Jack sat quietly. Linn began to fidget after a moment or two of his silence.

"There's more you want to say," he said. "What is it? Tell me," he urged with quiet reassurance. "I want to know. I won't run away."

"Well, on a more personal level," she began tentatively, "all this danger makes me feel weak and cowardly. I never feel that way in the operating room."

"You are anything but weak, Linn. Going skiing today may be a dumb idea. But you know how tired I am of living in fear. I've felt trapped." Reaching over, he touched the side of her face gently with his fingertips. "Being with you is good. I'm happy. Wiley's happy. It all means nothing if you're not happy."

"I'm not *unhappy*." She struggled to find the right words. "I love being with the two of you. The truth is, I'm scared of your occupation. I see the world through the eyes of a physician. I fix pain and suffering *after* it's been inflicted. If we go out today, are we baiting trouble to come and get us? Needless endangerment goes against everything I stand for and everything I do."

"You sound like a kind, loving friend. Thank you for telling me."

Offering her a tender smile he forced himself to go on, hating to say his next words, but the conversation was worthless if he didn't.

"I am a policeman. Things on my end are not going to change. Really, the big question is can you live with my chosen lifestyle? It's not easy to do. The stress of it has shattered the future for thousands of couples."

"I know. I want to try. I'm not a quitter."

Jack cleared his throat. Quid pro quo. It was his turn to come clean.

"Well, then here's my confession. Talking about my feelings is hard. I'll need your help to keep everything open and flowing between us so our disappointments don't escalate out of control.

"But I have a problem," he continued, finding it easier than he'd thought. "I can't keep hiding scary conversations from Wiley. When Annie died I al-most lost my son, too, because I cut myself off from feeling anything and that included Wiley. Ironically, zombies brought us back together."

Linn opened her mouth to speak, but Jack raised a hand.

"Trying to shield Wiley from danger feels like I'm cutting him out of my life again. Don't get me wrong. It's not easy telling him things that might keep him up at night, but he's been a part of this case from the beginning. I need to honor his intelligence and allow him to make some choices as we go forward."

Linn took a deep breath. "Yes, that makes sense. I wasn't seeing it from that angle." Squeezing Jack's hand gently, she ventured, "Can you understand my side of it at all?"

"Of course! I've known some of it, but I couldn't figure out how to start the conversation. I didn't want to hurt your feelings or lose what we've found."

Linn smiled, touched by Jack's thoughtfulness. "As Wiley's father, you should decide how to handle your relationship, but talking it out with me from time to time will help me understand."

"And not feel left out."

"Ah…yes," She replied awkwardly. Then her eyes widened with sudden comprehension, causing her to blush. "That's it exactly, isn't it? Exclusion. I hope that's not what Wiley's been feeling."

"He may have," Jack said, knowingly, as he thought back to the other afternoon in the kitchen.

"That's not good. We can do better," Linn said.

Delighted by the 'we,' Jack felt his clenched muscles unlock. "I can't wait to try," he whispered. Pulling her close, he kissed her with newfound hope. "What about today? How much time needs to pass before we believe we are safe? There was no trouble at the party. Grosse Ile has been zombie free for three months. Skiing or no skiing?"

"Put that way," she laughed, "skiing! I'm being silly. If the thing didn't show last night, why would it come after us today? What a relief! I needed this talk and your fabulous kiss! And now, kind sir, as I've heard Bridget call you, I'm ready for breakfast."

20

A CALL FOR HELP

Organizing eight people anxious to spend a day on the water turned out to be easy. By 10 a.m. the boats were fully loaded with skis, food (enough to last several days), drinks, towels, and beach chairs. For fun, the couples split up. Aboard Jack's beloved boat, *The Best Spot*, were Bridget, Brian, and Cameron. Steve's brand new Cobalt, *Can't Catch Me*, held Wiley, Libby, and Linn.

What was not easy was deciding where to go. White Sands, a first choice for years, was no longer an option. It was named for rolling dunes of white powder dredged and dumped on the end of Bois Blanc Island, and the former home of an Ontario, Canada amusement park called Boblo. The park closed its doors in 1993. Although the rest of the island was in use, the beloved white sand beach was now a no trespassing area.

At last they agreed to start at the Cross Dike. If it got too crowded they would find a new spot or move out on the lake.

"Hey, there's Clark," Steve yelled to Jack, as they made their approach.

They pulled alongside a slick cigarette boat and Molly, Clark's wife, broke into a broad grin. "Good morning!" she called happily. "Will you join us? I had a wonderful time last night. Thanks again for making it happen."

"It was our pleasure, Molly," Jack called back. "Anyone want to ski?"

"We do!" replied twelve-year-old Ginger with a huge grin. Her sister Camille, a year older than Wiley, nodded in agreement.

"Shall we eat first?" Clark inquired. "We can tie up together, have some lunch, and then if anyone wants to lounge we'll leave a boat and take the other two."

With nods from everyone, Jack and Steve threw in anchors. When the boats were connected they arranged themselves as desired on each other's decks.

Steve tried almost everything and was shoving the last of his sandwich in with his fingers when he stood up. Full of food and energy, he couldn't sit a minute longer.

"Who wants to go first?" he asked, as he started untying his boat from the others.

Bridget, Linn, and Molly offered to stay behind on the first round.

"Cameron," Wiley yelled over to the next boat, "do you want to go with me?'

"No. You like to go faster than I do."

Pointing to his chest with both hands, Brian called out, "Choose me... choose me!"

"Okay, I choose you!" The two clapped hands together in the air, knowing it would be great. They were well matched physically and athletically.

To lighten the load on Steve's boat, the teens unloaded coolers and other non-necessary equipment to *The Best Spot*. For the boys, especially, it was all about speed.

"You're okay with waiting to ski later?" Steve asked Bridget.

"Yes, I'm moving slowly and just want to lay here and soak up the sun for a while."

"It must be a girl thing," Steve mumbled softly, unable to imagine lying around when he could be skimming across the water with his heart thudding and his muscles primed.

"Hey, guys," Clark called, as the boats drifted apart. "What do you say, when everyone else has had their fill, we get the other boat and the three of us give it a go?"

"Definitely," Steve declared. "Jack? You up for it?"

"Heck, yeah!" Jack grinned slyly, sensing a challenge.

With a wave they left *The Best Spot* behind. Conditions for skiing were as close to perfect as you could get, which was rarely the case. Today the water was calm as glass. Many people were fooled, hurt, or killed on the Great Lakes each year, not realizing how dangerous they were due to their size. Often called inland seas, quickly changing conditions such as high winds, strong currents, and powerful waves caught amateur boaters off guard, with devastating results.

Wiley, in Steve's boat, and Brian, in Clark's, donned life jackets. Even though they all could swim, safety precautions were a must in case of injury. No one complained, as the ever evolving, lightweight designs were easy on the body.

When the boats were far enough away from any others they stopped to allow the kids to grab a slalom ski, throw it off the back, and jump in after it. They floated easily on their backs to pull on the ski and wait for the towrope.

"Hey, you two," Libby shouted. "Don't be pigs and hog the whole day just because we let you go first. We want our turn!"

"No problem." Wiley grabbed the towrope handle floating in front of him. "We promise to save you *at least* ten minutes!"

Cameron laughed. Brian gave a nod. Wiley punched his thumb up into the air. The two boats powered to life at the go signal. The motors rumbled deeply, generating a flourish of big, fat grins. Wiley and Brian sprang up out of the water and immediately crossed the wake line. Dancing across the surface of the amazingly smooth expanse of blue, their wet, taut bodies glistened in the sun.

Communicating your desires while skiing was simple. A mandatory sight person, someone other than the driver, kept an eye out to interpret the signals. Thumbs up by a skier meant go faster, thumbs down reduced the speed, a finger circling in the air indicted another round. A slash across the throat indicated the skier was calling it quits. Of course they could just let go of the rope.

Watching the boys was pure joy. The effort involved to do what they did was lost because they made it look easy. Wiley had learned the most demanding tricks from his mother when he was pretty young, and he and Brian had been practicing ever since.

"Feel the ache, Wiley," his mother had said, "and then keep trying until you're satisfied." Considering failure a good thing, Annie Davis had taught her son to test his strength and push the boundaries with exuberance.

The girls had changed out of bikinis into one-piece suits, knowing all too well how the drag of the water could pull off the skimpy pieces when they rose up out of the lake. After their turn, Ginger and Camille went next, and then all four girls did a round. When they'd had enough, Clark returned the kids to Steve's boat and picked up the women. The teens were happy to be left behind, already ravenous again from giving it their all.

The six adults were as thrilled as the kids to have a go. They could still put on an amazing show. The only reason Clark heard his phone ring was because they had stopped to changed skiers. His face turned dark with worry.

"Someone called in an anonymous tip to the dispatcher," he told Steve, Bridget, and Molly when he disconnected. "They saw a woman dragged from a car, then thrown over a man's shoulder while they were driving by a house on Thorofare. All available officers are being asked to report and help with the search."

"Get out, you two," Steve called down to Jack and Linn, who were in the water awaiting their turn. "The party's over."

"Wouldn't you know," Jack said, as he climbed out. He was seriously disappointed. When he heard the details he said, "And no one thinks it's suspicious the person calling in a kidnapping won't give their name? How legit can this be? And why do we have to go? There are people on duty for just this reason."

"You know we have a small police force and have to cover for each other. Wait a minute. Are you crying? There's *no* crying…" Steve started laughing.

"…in baseball!" Jack shouted back good-naturedly, quoting a favorite line from *A League of Their Own*.

• • •

Jack and Steve entered the police station forty-three minutes after Clark got the call to report. They were astonished to run into David Stryker, who was giving a statement about his misadventure the day before.

Clark, who had arrived seconds before them, shared what little information he'd learned. "You already know most of what happened to David. He was wandering the marina dock taking water samples and thought he smelled meth fumes coming from a pretty nice cruiser with navy trim. Peeking through a curtain, he saw ingredient remains lying on a table. That's all he can recall. The boat is long gone."

"Of course it is," Steve said, frowning. "I don't remember seeing it when we were there. Jack?"

"No, I don't either, but I didn't get close to the dock area. We'll keep an eye out for it. How is the kidnapping search being organized?"

"Sign in at the desk," Clark told them. "We're backup to Jessop and Steele who are currently at the property. They've put in for a warrant to search the property. It shouldn't be much longer until we're on the move."

Jack paced while they waited for further instructions. A call from Wiley surprised him.

"Hey, kiddo. What's up?"

"Dad," Wiley said, talking fast. "It's so weird! We found Sander Firth in the Wildlife Sanctuary. His mouth, eyes, arms, and legs were duct taped. We cut his arms and legs free."

"The Wildlife Sanctuary?" Jack was momentarily confused. "What are you and Brian doing there?"

"Everybody left so we took a bike ride. What do we do? Can you come?"

"Steve and I will be there within ten. Stay with him and try not to trample the area. We'll send an ambulance."

"Okay, but hurry! It's pretty spooky here in the woods."

21

LOST AND FOUND

When Jack and Steve were called into work, they gave Linn, Bridget, Brian, Libby, Cameron, and Wiley the option to take a boat and stay out on the water. The two women and four kids voted unanimously to return to the house.

Jack and Steve skipped helping unload and ran for the house to change. Like ships passing in the channel, those leaving and those coming slid by each other at the kitchen door.

After the women and kids unpacked the coolers and put away the dry supplies, the females quickly abandoned the males. Cameron and Libby wanted to play tennis and Linn needed to go home and pick up a few things. Bridget was going with her, wanting to see the construction progress since she'd last been at Linn's.

Left alone, Wiley and Brian were in the kitchen. Today things seemed a little less weird between them.

"Want one?" Wiley asked, his hand in the fridge.

"Yes." Snatching the flying can from the air, Brian thumped the container top hard two times before he pulled the tab. "Now what?"

"You still want to hang?" Wiley was suddenly nervous to be alone with Brian. He didn't want to hear another word about last night.

"Yup. If I go home and my mom hears about David, she'll be all over me and I'll never get out again."

"What about seeing if anyone wants to play the hitchhiking game?"

It was a game Wiley and Brian had made up. There wasn't much to do on Grosse Ile in the way of commercial activities. You had to go off Island for that, and since they were too young to drive, they pretty much had to invent their own fun.

The hitchhiking game was really an elaborate scavenger hunt. Everyone playing met in a designated place and divided into teams. Next they decided on a goal to go after, like collecting as many items as possible from a list or getting one big item that was a real challenge. Past ideas included acquiring a signed note from a teacher, or having your picture taken on a Jet Ski belonging to someone who was not currently playing. After agreeing on a grand prize, the teams took off walking in different directions. The best part of the game stemmed from the fact Grosse Ile was a contained community. You knew practically everyone. Sooner, usually than later, someone would drive by and offer you a ride. The key to winning was to persuade them to deliver you as close as possible to where you needed to go. A definite game changer was if you could convince them to wait for you and return you to the start. Bribes were not off limits. The first team back with the goods won.

"I don't know, it can take forever to organize, let alone play," Brian said, after giving it some thought. "Let's just ride."

Wiley nodded. "How about checking out the secret lab. The house is still empty."

"Okay. We can cruise the Wildlife Sanctuary. We haven't done that in a while."

They quickly stuffed two backpacks with drinks, food, and their phones. After riding off Hickory, they stayed on East River, taking their time as they headed north.

"Listen." Brian nodded as they passed Gray's Drive. "'Tis the season." They couldn't see the high school, but the marching band was rehearsing for the first game.

"Football is so flashy," Wiley said, a bit scornfully. "There are uniforms, cheerleaders, loud speakers, and big, loud drums!"

"So unlike the practically silent sport of rowing," Brian laughed. "But I've never wanted to play a contact sport."

"Me neither."

They rode as far as they could before East River bent to the left and its name changed to Horsemill. After about twenty yards, they turned at the first right onto Parke Lane. Nearing their friend Rick's driveway, they rode in even though he wasn't home. He and his family were away again for the weekend.

"What a place," Brian sighed. There was a pool, a trampoline, a tennis court and, although not on display, an assortment of water toys, both motorized and not, to satisfy any whim.

"No kidding," Wiley agreed, thinking of the Hydrobike in the boathouse. He loved the thing. It had a propeller and could go about five mph, even when the water was choppy. "But what a waste. They're never here to enjoy it. They're always busy, always on the run. If I had this, I'd hate to leave."

"Would you trade it for Sugar?"

"No way!" Wiley said, horrified by the idea.

Brian burst out laughing, and for that, he received a hard punch on his upper arm. "Hey!"

Their next stop, 2548 Parke Lane, was just up the road. The house had a curved driveway in front where they parked their bikes.

"You okay?" Brian half whispered, as they walked around the vacant building. Wiley's complexion had lost most of its color.

"This place is creepier than I thought," Wiley confessed. It was here, last spring, his father had been mauled by a zombie.

"Come on," Brian coaxed, "let's go."

They drifted farther north to Bridge Road where they went left again on Thorofare, then left again into the Wildlife Sanctuary. It was a pretty cool place to ride. A canopy of tree branches filtered out the hot sun overhead and they were walled in on each side by thick, dark woods. The road was dirt and had been recently oiled to keep down the dust. After dodging a sea of potholes, Wiley took advantage of a fairly smooth patch of road and pulled alongside his friend.

"Isn't there a bench along here somewhere?" he asked. "Let's stop. I'm dying of thirst."

Minutes later they found what they needed, and were sitting peacefully devouring several kinds of cookies made by Bridget.

"These are *so* good!" Brian was holding a handful of chocolate chip. "Remember when David was telling us about watershed areas and how they work? The other night my dad was saying this place, besides being a safe haven for birds and animals, is a part of the Lake Erie Watershed. Water from here drains into the Detroit River and goes south to Lake Erie."

"And it's partially cleaned by this wetland area," Wiley mumbled through a mouthful of peanut butter cookie.

"How can grass, dirt, and rocks clean junk from water?"

"It's magic!" Wiley laughed. "David told me he's been fighting to stop developers from filling in wetlands so they can build over them. It's illegal, but it still happens."

"You gotta love David!" Brian said sincerely. He stuffed one last cookie in his mouth before brushing crumbs from his shirt and hands. "My dad warned me spots in these woods can suck you in—like quicksand—after heavy rains."

"Really? Here?" Wiley frowned. "That's pretty scary. I've only heard this place is haunted."

"Haunted…yeah," Brian laughed. "Well, the quicksand-like thing only happens when clay gets waterlogged. It would have to be raining hard for days."

"Michigan is loaded with clay."

Brian nodded. He glanced at the dark wall of trees surrounding them. "You can be sure I'm not going in there to check it out."

Catching Brian by surprise, Wiley jumped up. His backpack hit the ground with a thump. "Did you hear something?"

"A cry? A hurt animal? Wait!" Brian yelled at his friend's back.

Just like yesterday on Sugar, Wiley bounded off toward the trees in search of an answer. After going about ten yards, he turned back and put his finger to his lips. "Shhh!" With his other arm he made a rolling motion for Brian to follow. "This way," he urged softly.

Brian hesitated. As he got to his feet his mind flashed warnings: quicksand, haunted woods, poison ivy…. Wiley was standing knee-deep in it. Brian was highly allergic. Just seeing it made him itch, but hoping for the best, he plunged in anyway not wanting to miss the adventure.

A definite moan came from their right. The deeper into the woods they went, the going got harder. The forest floor was filled with new growth and interlaced with last summer's foliage that crinkled and rustled under their feet. They stepped over several downed trees and branches, upsetting clouds of newly hatched mosquitoes that swarmed over them. When they stopped walking to listen, it was torturous. Flies and mosquitoes buzzed in their ears and covered their skin, no matter how much they slapped at their necks, faces, arms, and legs.

"Over there." He pointed at a dark mass huddled in the undergrowth and then spit out what had flown in when he'd opened his mouth. He took off running again, stopping so abruptly Brian crashed into his back. "I think it's Sander!"

As though released from a starting gate, the two bolted forward. A man, lying on his stomach with his face turned away, was almost completely covered by poison ivy. Walking around the body, they could see enough of the face to identify Sander, even though his eyes and mouth were covered with tape. He was breathing. What skin they could see glistened with plant oil and was covered with bright, red welts. His hands, bound tightly behind his back, were blue, the fingers swollen like sausages.

"Be right back." Brian was already moving. "I've got a knife in my pack."

"Run!" Wiley yelled. "And bring a phone!"

Sander lay lifeless. Bending over him, Wiley whispered, "Sander, it's Wiley. Can you hear me?" When the man did not respond, the boy gently shook his shoulder. "Sander?"

"Here you go." Brian was panting from his run. He held out a small Swiss Army knife.

"Hold his arms," Wiley said, "so they don't flop down when I make the cut. They must be stiff after being pulled tight and stuck in this weird position."

"Man, look at his hands! He must be in agony!"

The tape cut easily and Brian lowered each arm gently to the ground.

"I'm going to leave the rest of the tape wrapped around his wrists. He's arms are pretty hairy. Why torture him more by pulling it off? What do you think, should we roll him over? I shook his shoulder but he didn't move."

"I don't know," Brian said with a shrug. "Nothing looks broken, but aren't you supposed to call for help and not move someone who's injured?"

"Yes, but he's breathing poison ivy! Come on, grab his leg and I'll lift his shoulder. One, two, three…"

Sander moaned again as they shifted him onto his back.

"He's a mess," Brian said. "How are you going to get the tape off his mouth?"

"You mean without ripping his face off?"

Brian nodded.

"I'm not. Hand me the phone."

When Jack Davis answered, Wiley spoke so fast he had to repeat some of what he said to be understood. "Dad, it's so weird! We found Sander Firth lying in the Wildlife Sanctuary. His mouth, eyes, arms, and legs were duct taped. We cut his arms and legs free."

"The Wildlife Sanctuary?" Jack sounded momentarily confused. "What are you and Brian doing there?"

"Everybody left so we took a bike ride. What do we do? Can you come?"

"Steve and I will be there within ten. Stay with Sander and try not to trample the area. We'll send an ambulance."

"Okay, but hurry! It's pretty spooky here in the woods."

"Steve and my dad are coming," Wiley explained to Brian when he disconnected. "They're sending an ambulance."

"Wow," Brian said, trying not to sound pleased, "am I glad I didn't go home. I feel sorry for Sander, but look what I would have missed. We're two for two!"

"True! But what's it going to cost us? We're standing in poison ivy up to our knees. In shorts!"

• • •

After the ambulance picked up the still unconscious Sander, Wiley and Brian rode back to Hickory. Jack and Steve, more worried than ever over the fact Sylvia wasn't answering her phone, drove to the house she and her father shared. No one was home and there was no sign of trouble. Crawling into his Jeep, Jack clicked his seatbelt and started the engine.

"What?" Jack finally asked Steve, who was too quiet.

"Remember last spring Sander mentioned he had a sense not all the players in the zombie drama had surfaced? I think he was right. Sylvia is attached to her phone. She tells us all the time, 'call day or night.' Now she's not picking up and we can't find her. Besides that, people are disappearing and then being dumped like trash. I'm assuming all of this is related, but *why* escapes me. The only thing that makes sense is there must be another entity involved with a master plan."

"Someone embedded after all this time—I hate it, but it rings true."

"I also believe Sylvia going MIA and Sander's abduction have to do with the lost zombie."

Jack inhaled sharply. "Meaning our three months of peace and quiet are over, and the fun is about to begin."

"Again," Steve frowned.

After finding no clues or answers to any of their questions regarding Sylvia, they put in another appearance at the police station. The anonymous tip incident had fizzled out. No warrant had been issued. The judge could not be convinced that real harm was being done from the verbal description called into the dispatcher. There'd been no response when the police knocked on the doors of the residence. They found nothing odd when they circled the property, and received no answer to their calls.

Steve checked with the hospital. Sander was not awake and Sylvia didn't answer when Jack tried her again. With nothing left to do, by five o'clock they had rejoined the group already seated at the Davis kitchen table.

22

THE PRICE OF FAMILY

SUNDAY AFTERNOON, LABOR DAY WEEKEND

A relentless chirping near Sylvia's ear made her head ache. She tried to open her eyes, but couldn't. Her body hurt all over. Was it because she was lying on the ground? Why was she lying on the ground? Try as she might she couldn't sit up. Something was terribly wrong.

It all came back in a rush. She'd been snatched and thrown in a boathouse.

What had happened to her father?

Unable to see, speak, or move easily, she willed herself to stay calm and try to figure things out. It was a near impossible task to make her mind work coherently, she was using so much energy to just hold it all together and not freak out. Had she been asleep? More likely, she'd passed out from sheer terror. But for how long? Was it the same day? Sunday?

A slight rustle a small distance away reminded her she wasn't alone. Something was in here. With her! It wasn't mice or rats. The stink alone told her it was something larger and viler than small rodents. Even as a steady stream of clear liquid dripped from her nose, the smell got through. And what was that rattle? A chain? Heavy scraping kept starting and stopping.

Suddenly, her skin tingled. A shiver shot down her spine. She waited— her heart pounding loudly in her ears. Bile rose sharply in her throat, threatening to gush into her mouth like water from a broken pipe.

Rolling awkwardly onto her stomach, she put her lips on the floor and rubbed them back and forth against the rough surface to remove the tape. When she could stand it no more, she raised her head. The skin around her mouth pinched painfully. She tried again, rubbing harder. One end pulled free. Immediately a stream of green sludge spurted out from the corner of her mouth. It dribbled down her chin onto her chest. The force of the second wave of sick coursing up from her stomach blew the rest of the soggy mess completely off, taking with it most of what little skin she had left on her lower face.

Sylvia spit to clear her mouth, but the sour taste stayed with her. She still couldn't see. Without the use of her eyes to evaluate the nuances of light, Sylvia had no sense of time.

She woke again smelling of vomit. One end of the tape that had covered her mouth dangled from her cheek. Lying flat on her back, sick with fear, she called to her mother. "You were afraid of just this thing happening, weren't you? That's why you kept yourself hidden all those years. Oh, if you could see me now. I've blown everything you worked so hard for, and I'm so sorry."

And her father? Maybe that was the worst part of this nightmare, she had no idea if he was dead or alive.

A sob escaped, without her even knowing it had formed. But doing nothing would not get her out of here. She needed to move…she must try, but every ounce of her wanted to just lay there and feel sorry for herself. Before her mind could react her body went rigid.

"Oh, *Syl-v-ia!*"

It was the driver. She'd not heard his approach. Rocking onto her side, she pulled herself into a ball as best she could to hide her mouth. Although she felt afraid, she was surprised to find the arrival of another human slightly lessened her feeling of desperation. *Surely* a person—a recognizable enemy—was better than the *other* unidentified one in the room.

"My dear," the voice said sweetly. So sweetly, it made Sylvia's stomach turn. "My friend and I have an assignment for you and we will help. By now you must realize you have a companion. Have you met? In just a moment the tape will be removed from your eyes and arms. I see you have already done so to your mouth. How was that experience?"

Sylvia did not reply.

"Probably pretty painful," the driver continued. "What a shame." Strong hands grabbed her arms and squeezed. "This might hurt a bit. Ready?"

Bound as she was, an attempt to resist was laughable. But she squirmed until a punch in her stomach doubled her over. A hand, sliding down the back of her head grabbed a thick chunk of her hair and pulled her face skyward. The skin around her eyes flamed in pain as the tape was ripped away. Hot tears poured down her face. Her unbound arms flopped heavily to the floor. Forced to sit up, a cold, wet washcloth smelling of river water was placed into her right hand. Her arms wobbled uncontrollably as she spread it open and lifted it to her oozing facial wounds.

When the cloth hurt more than it helped, she threw it in her lap. The room and its occupants were blurry, hazy, and the legs of the two men standing near her blocked much of her view. After observing what she could of her surroundings, Sylvia squared her shoulders and looked directly at what she'd been avoiding in the corner opposite her. A zombie was chained to the wall by its ankle. The cruelty shook her deeply.

"Now," the driver instructed harshly, his mouth tight against her ear, "you will insert a microchip into the back of this creature's head." He chuckled wickedly. "Don't worry, he won't feel a thing!"

As she tried to process what she was being forced to do, the men left her momentarily and approached the creature. One carried two blankets. After dropping them on the floor, he cautiously grabbed the top of the chain near the wall. Pulling it tight, the zombie's foot came up off the floor, forcing it off-balance. The driver, standing ready, grabbed a blanket and threw it over the thing's head. The second man dropped the chain, grabbed the extra blanket, and threw it on top of the first. Both men wrestled the creature to the ground. It took practically a whole roll of tape to secure the material around the thing's chest. Next they taped its legs together, before cutting the blankets around the neck, freeing the creature's head. The makeshift straitjacket held, no matter how hard the zombie wiggled.

The driver grabbed Sylvia. "Here is the chip. Hold out your hand."

Sylvia's arm shook erratically. Unable to hold her hand steady, she dropped the tiny apparatus. It bounced away, the driver swore, and scurried to retrieve it. This time he placed it in the palm of her hand, closed her fingers tightly around it, and yanked her to him. From his pocket he removed a handgun and held it against her temple. "I'm going to give you a scalpel. If you make any move to attack the creature or us, I will shoot you. Understand?"

"I don't…," Sylvia coughed, her raw throat was closed tight with fear.

"…have any experience?" the same man finished. His ugly laugh was chilling.

Sylvia nodded. It was the best she could do.

"Experience isn't necessary. Let me be clear, *Syl-v-ia*. As you have probably noted, your options are limited. You will do this. Be quick and get it done!"

The two men stepped away when Sylvia took possession of the scalpel. The creature was on its stomach at her feet. Its head, sticking out of the blankets, resembled a turtle's protruding from its shell. A heavy hand thumped onto her shoulder, pushing her down onto her knees. The room whirled as a wave of dizziness washed over her. She tried not to gag. The repulsive stench was overwhelming.

The driver kneeled down, placed a hand on each side of the creature's head, and twisted it sideways so its cheek rested on the floor. The second man planted his foot on the creature's exposed ear and pressed down, pinning its head to the floor. He quickly rearranged his hands, cradling the creature's chin in one and putting the other behind its head in a vice-like grip.

Without pausing to think, Sylvia put her left hand on the zombie's neck and made a horizontal slit about an inch long. Her mind registered the lack of blood, and for that blessing she was most thankful.

"The skin is so thick and rubbery!" she croaked in surprise. She wore no gloves. *And cold*, she thought to herself. The chip slid easily into the flesh. With stiff fingers she pinched the flaps of skin together and turned and looked at the driver, whose face was just inches from hers.

Removing his hand from the zombie's chin, the driver took a curved, threaded needle from his pocket. He handed it to Sylvia and gripped the creature's chin again.

The tug of each stitch rocked the zombie's head and turned Sylvia's stomach. After tying off the last knot she rose shakily.

The three humans, amazed and transfixed by the success of the procedure, stood back in awe.

It was the wrong move.

At the release of the pressure holding it down, the creature threw back its head and arched its back. Several of the constraining straps of tape popped from around its chest. Eager hands pulled off the rest, and it was on its feet. Extending its trapped leg away from the wall until the chain became taut, it jerked hard. The chain held. The ankle bone snapped. The metal band slid down, but not off. The foot dangled uselessly, still attached to its leg by a few tendons. With a swift swat the zombie sent the foot flying across the room. The metal band, sliding free, clanked loudly onto the floor.

In four hops the creature was at the boat slip. It grabbed the handrail and twisted around to examined Foley and Moreno with its damaged, weeping eyes. Next it let go of the rail and hopped again, landing two feet shy of Sylvia. Unable to catch its balance, it fell down on all fours. It lifted its head to stare, but made no move to hurt or help her. Foley, Moreno, and Sylvia stood frozen until it scampered clumsily to the boat slip where it entered the water with such grace there was no splash.

This time Sylvia didn't black out completely from her emotional overload. She browned out. Her personal energy voltage was sharply reduced, like electricity in a bad storm. Her trauma left her looking awake and as though nothing was wrong, but dropped her to the floor in a stupor.

When her catatonic state broke and her senses returned, she was sitting in a pool of urine. Slow to respond, she rose stiffly, amazed to find she was alone, unrestrained, but still locked in the boathouse. She thought about following the zombie's example and swimming to freedom. But in her pathetic condition, she might drown. She was a lousy swimmer.

Taking off her shorts, she made her way to the slip. Contemplating the water, she reconsidered diving in, but couldn't make herself do it. Instead, she rinsed her shorts in the river, wrung them out, and put the clammy things back on before going to sit against the wall near the entrance used by the two men.

It was impossible to get comfortable, she ached all over. Forcing herself to ignore the pain, she reviewed as much as she could remember about being abducted. Certainly, this incident had taught her the most valuable lesson of her life. She really was cursed. The hard truth was she'd been so before she'd learned of her heritage, she was now, and would be forever.

Her screaming changed nothing.

• • •

It swam slowly through the narrow confines of the canal until the dark brown water turned clear. In a dance of jubilation and rehydration it twisted, jumped, and rolled over in the open water. Farther and farther from shore it went, diving deeper and deeper—reveling in its freedom.

But the urgent stinging, buzzing in its head would not stop. Treading water, it shook its body frantically. Nothing helped. It had to respond.

Re-entering the confines of the canal, it nosed its way under moored boats and around sunken logs and dock pilings to the boathouse. There, it settled on the mucky bottom among the grasses across from its recent prison, fighting the command to come closer and make a full return.

• • •

23

LINN'S HOUSE

SUNDAY AFTERNOON, LABOR DAY WEEKEND

Linn and Bridget dropped the girls at Cameron's, made a fast stop on Macomb, and then turned north.

"What's changed since I was last there?" Bridget asked excitedly, once they were alone.

"Tons. You can see it all."

Eight months ago, before she met Jack, Dr. Linn Erickson had serendipitously moved to Grosse Ile and bought a house on Knudsen Drive in Potawatomi Woods. The spacious backyard butted the east side of the canal, which was really a diverted part of the Detroit River. The modest 1950's ranch had been carefully deconstructed, and was now being artfully renovated. Bridget had pored over the speculative drawings and loved what she's seen. Watching it all come to life was a kick.

Viable materials from the gutted structure were being reused by the contractor or donated for resale. Recycled products would be incorporated where possible. Low energy and green innovations like a metal roof to capture the sun's heat, foam insulation to keep the structure's interior temperate in summer and winter, and replacing the standard water heater with a coil system were a few of the solutions being activated. A new glassed-in, covered walkway on the side of the house would serve as a porch and a connection to a sunroom being added at the back. Solar panels covering the roof would defray the cost of maintaining some of the luxuries like the hot tub.

"I vote drinks on the deck," Linn said, as she parked in the driveway. "Come into the kitchen with me. Then if you'll go set out the cushions, I'll be right behind you."

"Happy to…" Bridget replied.

After showing her around, Linn handed Bridget two beach towels and slid open the French doors. Bridget stepped outside onto a handsome slate walkway. Between the stones something wonderful had been planted that omitted a pungent, delectable odor when her sandals brushed against it. The path meandered through the dappled shade of three huge maple trees, where the thick trunks were encircled by dark green Empress Wu Giant Hostas. The plants' huge leaves intertwined thickly, giving a jungle feel to the space. Like a circle of fire below, bright red begonias provided sharp contrast at ground level.

The sun kissed Bridget's face the minute she emerged from under the trees. Bold color was plentiful. The heady scent of red, orange and yellow roses enveloped her as she stopped to watch bees and blue, red, yellow, and black dragonflies dance from flower head to flower head.

Next came a riparian buffer about a yard wide, planted between the shoreline and the mowed lawn. Root systems of native grasses, shrubs, flowers and a few small, flowering trees would slow down storm-water runoff into the canal, filter pollutants and reduce erosion, while providing a habitat for wildlife.

Ignoring the handsome furniture and her assigned task of arranging cushions, Bridget walked to the front of the deck, folded one of the towels she was holding, and sat down. Below her, peat-colored water, so different from the green-blue at Jack's, glistened with what was probably motor oil. After kicking off her sandals she touched the water's surface with a toe, sending bugs skating gracefully away. The bottom wasn't visible; she could see down only about eight to ten inches. Close to shore where there was no boat traffic, she saw clumps of algae and the tops of water plants reaching out and waving with the current. Idly she wondered what lived down below what was visible.

The width of the canal was maybe sixty yards, but she wasn't sure of her measurements. The surrounding backyards offered a stupendous, and much more interesting view of neighborhood life than any front yard. From previous visits she knew almost every homeowner owned at least one boat, but today most of the slips were empty. She felt a slight tinge of disappointment at not being able to feast her eyes on the magnificent displays. She had expected it, as this was the last holiday weekend of the summer and Michigan's boating season was short. Still, she felt the loss.

At last she found the cushions under a counter cabinet. She settled comfortably on a handsome chaise lounge—one she was certain she recognized from a magazine ad—and waited for Linn.

Directly across from her two men stood talking in the middle of a yard. She waved when they looked over. The old grumps stared for a minute, before averting their eyes and scurrying into a large, screened-in porch.

'Fraidy cats', she laughed to herself. But she jumped when Linn called to her.

"Sorry I took so long! I stupidly answered the phone. It was my mother, loaded with good news which I was glad to hear, but I couldn't get off." In each hand Linn held a giant, plastic drink cup.

"What have you brought me?" Bridget laughed in surprise. She took a quick sip from the straw of the pre-offered drink. "Um, this is good!"

"A treat, just for us." Linn pulled her lounge closer to Bridget. "What about the umbrella? Is it too hot? It's easy to put up."

"No," Bridget said with a shake of her head, "the sun feels great. This is some place you've found. But what's with your neighbors?" She gestured at the house across the water. "I think my presence scared them back into their house."

"Who needs them?" Linn smirked as she lowered the back of the chair, spread her towel, and stretched out fully. "I haven't met them. They moved in after I did and built that monstrous boathouse."

"Well, they sure weren't inclined to make a new friend of me. How are things going with you and Jack? You're still interested?"

"I am very interested in Jack Davis," Linn grinned. "We had a heart-to-heart this morning and cleared up a bunch of confusion. He told me statistically it's pretty rough to date a cop and I admit his profession scares me. What about you and Steve? How's that going?"

"I fell for him the moment we met. I'm pretty happy."

After laughing together at their good fortune, Linn laid her head back and closed her eyes. "Aren't we the lucky pair?"

"What the heck?" Bridget cried. A tremendous, and totally unexpected splash drenched both women. Jumping to her feet in part surprise, part outrage, she looked around wildly. "Did someone cannonball us?"

Both women scurried to the front edge of the deck. Right below them the churning water of the canal was cloudy with bottom silt.

"Something's down there." Linn's voice was a whisper.

"Something big."

"Leave the cushions and let's go," Linn instructed, tugging gently on Bridget's arm.

"I'm right behind you," Bridget told her. But actually, she was first off the dock and first back on land.

24

DINNER IS SERVED

SUNDAY EVENING, LABOR DAY WEEKEND

When Jack and Steve arrived home from the station, Linn, Bridget, Wiley, and Brian were sitting at the kitchen table, filling each other in on their afternoons. The detectives were in time to hear Brian describe finding Sander.

"Luckily for him, he was still unconscious when the EMTs pulled the tape off his mouth. But he threw up anyway. I didn't know you could do that," Brian told the assembled group. His eyes sparkled with excitement, now that the danger was past. "It was pretty grim. He'd been lying in poison ivy; it was everywhere! Can't you picture his face covered in blisters the size of quarters?" Brian threw his hands hopelessly in the air. "Poison ivy loves me…."

Linn had written a prescription for a fast pack of prednisone for both boys after learning how unprepared they'd been for their adventure in the woods.

"It hates me too, Brian." Steve said, frowning. "It's becoming a menace. Global warming's increased carbon monoxide levels work like an elixir on the plants. They're experiencing an unprecedented surge in growth. Scientists predict the plants of today will grow into shrubs in the near future. Vines of the stuff already cover everything like Kudzu. What makes it so dangerous to humans is its oil doesn't readily dry up like water when exposed to air. If a dog runs through a field and leaf oil gets on its fur, the animal carries it around, spreading poison long after initial contact."

Wiley, who'd been petting Parker under the table, jerked his hand away.

"Linn and I had an interesting experience," Bridget said next. "We were sitting on her deck by the canal and out of the blue we got drenched by a zombie sized splash!" Reaching across the table, she selected a huge potato chip from a bowl.

"Zombie sized? What makes you say that?" Steve asked. He was watching Bridget intently as she submerged the chip in onion dip and put the whole thing in her mouth.

"She's kidding," Linn said, brushing aside the unwelcome reference with her hand.

Bridget nodded, swallowed, and then smiled. "I am, but it was freaky. There was so much water and the water below us churned madly."

"Think back carefully," Jack said. "What else did you notice?"

"We didn't see anything besides swirling water." Linn gave him an odd look. "But we didn't hang around."

"Between the underwater ruckus and the 'Fraidy cat neighbors," Bridget said, dismissively, "there was no reason to stay."

"Are these the new neighbors across the canal? Have you met them?" Jack asked, not willing to let go of the subject so easily.

"Not yet," Linn said. "I think they moved in sometime late winter or early spring." Suddenly, her eyes widened with recognition. "You don't really suspect something's fishy at my house, do you?"

"I think Sander lying unconscious in the hospital, while Sylvia isn't answering her phone, is very fishy. But I have a reason for asking about your neighbors. Isn't this the place with the new boathouse?" Jack asked. "That's where the anonymous tip about the kidnapping led us."

"Is this about Sander and Sylvia, or the boathouse?" Linn asked shrewdly. She watched Jack's face carefully for a reaction.

"Can't it be both?" Steve said, with a slight shrug of his shoulder.

"Just how deep is the canal?" Bridget reached for another chip.

"The depth varies, as does the murkiness," Jack answered her. "You might or might not see something even in shallow water. Can either of you think of a way the new neighbors, Sylvia, and the boathouse could be connected?"

"Don't forget the zombie," Wiley added.

For reasons unknown, everyone found this very funny.

"You know what sounds fishy to me," Steve joked, "is two guys running away when a beautiful brunette waves at them!"

"A *beautiful* brunette? Oh, that sounds nice. Tell me more!" Bridget begged playfully.

Jack finally smiled, but by the time he slid his cell phone from his pocket, his eyebrows were scrunched together in concentration.

"Who's out on patrol?" he asked the police dispatcher. "Okay, have them drive by the house on Thorofare again. Also, have them go into Dr. Erickson's backyard at 4714 Knudson. Right. Her house is directly across the water. Yes, I have her okay." Turning on the charm, he winked at Linn across the table. "I want to know the results ASAP. Thanks."

"You have my approval?" Linn raised an eyebrow.

"Too big a stretch?" Jack's eyes shone mischievously. "I figured you'd speak up if it really wasn't okay."

"Detective Davis, you do love to take liberties."

"How true, Dr. Erickson, how true."

Jack felt his mood lighten. The sudden occurrence of too many coincidences meant they were beginning to discover links. Finding, testing, and taking action were what Jack loved most about his job.

After dinner, the group voted unanimously for a board game night. Wiley and Brian invited the girls over and the dining room table was cleared. Two different options for play were available, one at each end of the table, and they would be run simultaneously. The winner of game #1 got to choose which opponents to play next. The winner of game #2 got to choose the game. They would play a total of three rounds.

"Yeah!" Brian cheered around 10 o'clock, when he was crowned Supreme Winner/King of the Games! Bridget was runner-up. The two biggest losers, Linn and Jack, were sent to the kitchen to find them all some dessert.

"I want an ice cream float," Brian boldly called after them, making use of his newly-won status. He had to act fast. Any perks from the honor would be short lived.

"Absolutely! I'll take orders," Bridget purred with pleasure. "Girls? What's your pleasure?"

"I'll have a chocolate shake," Cameron said, "and come help."

At ten of eleven, Jack drove each girl home. When he got back, everyone was in the living room waiting to watch Jimmy Fallon. Barring any new police developments, in the morning they were going skiing.

25

GATHERING THE BITS AND PIECES

VERY EARLY MONDAY MORNING, LABOR DAY

Jack was lying flat on his back staring at the ceiling. It was 4:10 a.m. He'd been awake for at least two hours worrying about Sylvia. Outside, a large portion of the insect population was keeping him company with their trilling, buzzing, and chirping. He loved the sounds of the night. He'd heard no owls, and their absence reminded him the Red Wing Blackbirds, the first to arrive in spring and the first to go, had left town for the winter. The big birds (herons, swans, and cranes) were still around, and because so much of the downriver area was now environmentally protected, there were a lot of them to enjoy. A cat meowed loudly, asking to come inside. Then, without knowing it, he began to make a mental list of fall chores: clean the gutters and storm windows, put the gardens to bed, rake the leaves, and this year there would be two boats to winterize.

He was almost glad when his phone rang.

"Jack Davis."

"Detective Davis, this is Josie Evans from Henry Ford Hospital in Wyandotte. I'm calling about Sander Firth. He woke up screaming a little while ago. He says his daughter has been kidnapped. He promised to calm down if I called you."

"Is he still awake?" Jack was out of bed heading toward his clothes.

"Yes. He wants to see you."

"I'm on my way. Give me twenty minutes."

"Stop at the front desk. I'll call down and expedite clearance. He's on the 4th floor, room 4223."

"Thank you." Jack threw the phone on the bed to zip and belt his pants. Then he crept down the hall and woke Steve, who he heard snoring through the guest room door. After a quick pit stop in the bathroom, Jack was downstairs writing a note when Steve entered the kitchen.

"Does this feel a little Deja vu to you?" Jack's car was blocked in so Steve drove.

"Except it's not about me being hospitalized," Jack chuckled. His voice carried in the quiet of the early morning. "But look at our luck from the last go around. You met Bridget and I met Linn."

"True," Steve beamed. "It's pretty nice, huh?"

"It's great." Capitalizing on their few minutes alone, Jack caught Steve up on his personal life. "Linn and I talked through a bunch of things yesterday morning."

Jack was looking out his window, his face turned away from Steve. It was still dark, another reminder fall was here. The early morning light of Daylight Savings Time, such a glorious gift in March after the long, dark Michigan winters, was waning. Today the sun wouldn't rise until after 6:30 a.m.

"Like?" Steve prompted.

"How hard it is to be in a relationship with a cop. What we do scares her."

Steve snorted. "Heck, it scares me."

"I told her how hard it is sometimes for me to share what I'm feeling. It's not exactly my strong suit." Jack smiled self-consciously.

"You and Annie used to do it."

"We did. Yesterday I managed to explain I can't keep hiding conversations from Wiley, like we did on Friday when he came home from school."

"Yes, why have you been doing it?"

"Linn thought the scary stuff might be too much for Wiley. I hadn't realized how afraid I'd become to talk straight with her until I got started. Then I kind of liked it. Things have been so good. I didn't want to spoil anything with her. Now, I'm worried I might have messed up things with Wiley."

"Is he acting differently?" Steve asked, surprised. He hadn't noticed any changes in the boy.

"No, but I just have this feeling."

Steve said nothing more until he'd turned left off of East River onto Groh Road. At Meridian he drove straight to the Toll Bridge. It would take them across into Wyandotte, just minutes from Henry Ford Hospital.

"Here's what I think regarding Wiley. Please remember he's a kid and you're the adult. Holding back some information is okay. You get to make that call. Furthermore, you haven't lied to him; you've just not told him everything. Having come clean with Linn, you can do the same with your son. Explain to Wiley what's happened, how it came about, and how it makes you feel. Let him know both *his* opinion and *Linn's* are important to you, but don't let him think Linn is calling the shots. That's not the case is it?"

"No." Jack turned to look at Steve. "And she doesn't want to. You think that will do it? I just want to make all the pieces work and feel good about it."

"Wiley and Linn care about you, and they care about each other. By bringing your concerns out in the open with each of them you can't go wrong."

"You make it sound so easy," Jack said, as they pulled into the hospital parking lot.

As they got out of the car, Jack thought about his wife and longed to talk to her. *Oh, Annie.* For a second she was there with him, smiling and shaking her head at what she would consider his foolishness. She had always understood him, and feeling her warmth and love once again was exquisite.

"Well, so far so good," Jack murmured softly, as they made their way into the huge hospital complex. "Please, don't let it all blow up in my face."

• • •

"Role reversal," Sander said wearily as the detectives entered the room. He tried to smile. "You visiting me here."

His face was swollen like a balloon, the skin tight, beet red, and raw. Under the fluorescent lights it shone eerily, thanks to a thick layer of yellowish salve slathered on his face, neck, and arms. His body looked frail and listless. Two pillows propped him up. There was no sign of his usual, extreme energy.

"Why can't we reach Sylvia?" Jack asked, not acknowledging Sander's preamble. "She's not picking up her calls."

"You've not found her? We were abducted." Sander's right eye began to twitch. "I am sick with worry. Two men tricked us yards from our house on Elba Island. They must think Sylvia knows something. We've got to find her." Sander threw back the sheet and blanket on the bed.

"No, no, no!" Jack said, hurriedly. "You are in no shape to start a search and rescue. Tell us what happened and send us on our way."

Sander had little to share. By the time he finished, his voice was barely audible.

"Sleep," Steve told him. "We know you want to help. We'll try and spring you from here later this morning, *if* the doctor thinks you can handle it."

Sander did as told and settled back down. He was asleep before the detectives left the room.

"Did I look that bad?" Jack wanted to know as soon as the door closed behind them. He'd lost two weeks of active duty healing in the hospital when he'd tangled with a zombie—and lost.

"Far worse," Steve said, honestly.

A small shudder shivered down Jack's spine. Memories…

At the car, Steve's cell rang. It was 5:10 a.m. and it was Clark on duty at the police station. "There's an abandoned boat anchored near Celeron Island. A fisherman called in a description that fits the one David saw at the marina. If you want it, it's yours to investigate."

"We want." This, Steve knew without asking, would be Jack's wish.

"Good. Do you want to go see it first before it's towed?"

"Hang on, let me ask Jack."

"You're together?" Clark asked, amazed. "Where are you?"

"Just leaving Henry Ford. Sander woke up agitated and a nurse called us. We were just going to text you. He and Sylvia were abducted yesterday.

She really is missing."

"What? You got details?"

"A few. Okay, Jack wants to try and get David to go with us to ID the boat. He'll call David while I send you a report on Sander and Sylvia. If all goes well and we get hold of him, out and back shouldn't take more than two hours. Then, we want to try and get Sander released. He should be a part of this, but he looked awful and seemed exhausted. It was hard to tell about his stamina. We left word for his doctor to sign him out if he's good to go."

"I'll look for your info."

Jack's call woke David. "Yes, I definitely want to join you." He lived about 35 minutes from Grosse Ile in Ypsilanti. "I can be there by 6:10 latest."

They took *The Best Spot*. Steve's prediction about an easy out and back inspection trip proved faulty. The morning was full of delays. David was willing—but much less able to get moving as quickly as he'd thought, so they didn't get away from the Davis dock until 6:40 a.m.

The boat was easy to spot, anchored about twenty feet out from Celeron's shore. They circled first, then made a slow approach.

David was adamant from the first. "That's it."

"Hello," Jack called loudly as they came around the vessel for the second time. When they were within thirty feet he put the motor in neutral and they drifted closer. "Anyone aboard?"

Exquisitely outfitted with the best of the best, the navy-blue trimmed vessel was gorgeous. The silence eerie.

"You know," Steve said softly, "if I didn't know better, I'd swear I just got a whiff of formaldehyde."

"Are you sure?" Jack inhaled deeply. "I don't smell anything."

Steve shrugged. "No, it could be my imagination."

"That would be good. I hope to never smell it again." Jack moved the gear back into forward. "There's definitely no one home."

Jack inched the boat forward enough for Steve to lean and grab the side of the other vessel before he cut the engine. Steve stepped onto the other boat's deck, holding *The Best Spot's* bow line. Jack placed two boat fenders over the side, threw Steve the rear line, and climbed on board.

"Hang on, David," Jack said, when he rose to join them. "Let us check it out first. Who knows what we'll find."

Steve pulled plastic gloves from his pocket and put them on before he tried the cabin door handle. It was locked. "Your call, Jack."

"My gut says something's not right, that's for sure. It could take forever for the Coast Guard to get here due to the holiday. And, if by some weird chance Sylvia's in there? We can't risk it. We'll have some explaining to do, but I say go for it."

Steve took a deep breath and shoved his shoulder hard against the door.

"Yikes!" Jack exclaimed, as the splintering wood of the doorframe cracked like a gunshot. "Watch somebody call the cops on us!" he joked darkly.

Inside they tried not to gag. The slovenly remains of human habitation completely ruined the once stately look of the interior. Used coffee filters, funnels, and a propane cylinder were strewn on the counter next to a small galley stove. Pots and pans, encrusted with black crud sat on burners covered in slop. An empty ice chest and discarded chemical containers were scattered all over the floor.

Talking soft and fast, the two missed seeing David peek inside from the doorway.

"Turn around you guys and get out," he told them, feeling his eyes start to burn from the fumes. "The place is contaminated and none of us are dressed correctly to come a calling."

"Right behind you," Jack said, nodding in agreement. "We'll call this in and get it towed. Leaving it out here unattended is way too dangerous."

Steve, last through the door, grabbed something from a seat at the kitchen table.

"My hat!" David exclaimed, when they were back on *The Best Spot* and Steve showed him what he'd found. It was an old, tattered baseball cap emblazoned with the distinctive *D* of the Detroit Tigers.

"If I can get reception out here," Jack said, as he pulled the anchor, "we may know the boat owner before we get back."

Once they were underway it took him two tries to get through. The

Coast Guard promised a callback ASAP regarding the ownership.

"Sander is cleared for release," Steve reported when he finished his call. "What do you say, David, we drop you off at Jack's. We'll get Sander and bring him back to the house to brainstorm."

"Brainstorming sounds great, but why don't we just keep going to the hospital? It's a straight shot from here and it sits right on the river. Surely you can tie up somewhere. I'll wait on the boat while you sign him out. Having to go all the way around Grosse Ile to drop me off first will waste time, and I've already delayed you while trying to get my act together this morning. You need to get him and start searching for Sylvia."

"Sound all right with you?" Jack asked Steve.

"It does."

At the hospital they were met with confusion over whether the doctor had signed his patient out. He had. It turned out Sander was in better condition than he looked, considering he'd been discarded and left to die. Once it was established he could leave, they were delayed by a pile of paperwork. They finally stepped outside at 10:15 a.m.

Initially, Sander was frazzled. Anxiety over his daughter's situation made him desperate to start searching for her right away. Jack tried to explain they would be best served if they devised a plan. The boat ride proved therapeutic and helped calm Sander's nerves.

"David, what do you have on for today?" Jack asked. To get from the hospital in Wyandotte to Jack's, they crossed the water north of the Island. It was windy, but *The Best Spot* cut through the whitecaps with ease.

"No plans. My day is wide open."

"The knot on your head still looks bad," Steve said.

"It's huge. I feel okay. Good, not great."

"Speak up if anything changes," Jack told him with a smile. "Today, medical attention at our house is pretty easy to obtain. There's both a nurse and doctor there!"

"Why don't you go in and rest," Steve said. "Maybe get something to eat. Jack and I will take Sander to the station. We shouldn't be long, then we'll meet you back at the house."

"That works," David replied.

After they docked, Jack walked David to the door to make sure he could get inside, and Steve took Sander to the car.

"I'm not sure who's here," Jack explained to David, "but you know everyone. Make yourself at home. Eat, drink anything you want. There are some good leftovers!"

At the station, Sander went through the events of the abduction. A police artist made several sketches of the two men, one far more detailed than the other. Sander had not gotten a real good look at the guy who snuck up and grabbed him. Still, there was more to go on than before. The sketches were scanned and distributed online within minutes.

By now Sander was dragging. It was 10:52 a.m. and everyone needed something to eat. As Steve popped the car's locks, Jack's phone rang.

It was Wiley.

"Hey kiddo," Jack said, coolly. But his heart rate picked up noticeably. "What's up?"

26

DOING THEIR OWN THING

MONDAY MORNING, LABOR DAY

Wiley was bored. He'd gotten up early expecting to go skiing, but found a note in the kitchen from his father instead. He and Steve were out doing detective stuff concerning David Stryker.

"Ah, man…" he sighed. His dad's notes were such fun crushers.

Linn and Bridget were at the table. Seeing Wiley's disappointment, Linn offered, "Bridget and I are going to do some fast shopping. Want to come?"

"Yes, join us," Bridget's eyes shone with interest. "We can look for something cool for school."

"Thanks anyway," Wiley replied feebly. He felt bad saying no, but shopping? He hated shopping. "I think I'll stay here. This is my last day of freedom before school starts tomorrow and I kind of want to be outside."

"We hear you," Bridget said, nodding with understanding as she stood up. "See you in a few."

As soon as the door closed and the house went silent, Wiley had a brilliant idea. Grabbing his phone he initiated a flurry of texts.

Wiley to Brian: <Skiing is off, at least for now. Dad's working. Want to go in the boat? Home by lunch in case skiing happens.>

Brian to Wiley: <Yes. With the girls?>

Wiley to Brian: <Yes. You text Lib, I'll text Cameron.>

Wiley to Cameron: <Skiing off this morn. Dad working. Brian and I want to go out with you and Lib. Interested?>

Cameron to Wiley: <I'm at Libby's. Sounds good. Now?>

Wiley to Cameron: <Now.>

Brian to Wiley: <Lib's a go. Cameron is with her. There in 15.>

Deciding to not bother with a bunch of stuff, Wiley was at the dock in plenty of time to meet everyone.

"Wiley, you recued me! I owe you!" Libby called from the lawn. She was drinking a Pepsi and carrying a beach towel. "My parents wanted me to help them 'whip the yard into shape' this morning. Hel-lo! Today is Labor Day, a holiday created to celebrate those of us who work very hard during the rest of the year. This is more like it!" Within seconds she jumped on board, stowed her stuff inside the front bench seat, turned around, and sat down ready for action.

Cameron was right behind her. Wiley helped her with her things. "Any requests where you want to go?" He was psyched! The outing had come together so easily. He was with his friends and not confined in the house.

"I liked Saturday's spot." Cameron waited for Wiley to take his seat behind the steering wheel, then she sat down next to him.

"To the other side of Sugar." Wiley turned the key and the motor came alive. He looked at Brian, who gave him a mock salute, then threw in the bow line, and pushed them away from the dock.

"I like being out so early in the day," Cameron said, looking around.

The night had been cool, in the low 50's, so the air was thick with moisture. The kids all wore shorts and sweatshirts. Although heavy clouds and possible rain were expected overnight, it was clear now, except for a light mist. It hung in spots, about ten feet above the water, blurring the colors and softening the shapes.

When they rounded the southern tip of Sugar they were surprised again to see there was no one else around.

"Nice," Brian said. "I love having the place to ourselves."

"Can't last!" Wiley commented.

They were about fifty feet out chugging north, when a hard knock against the bottom of the boat near the bow tipped them violently to the right. Wiley, Cameron, and Libby watched open-mouthed as Brian flew off the front seat, landing hard on his hands and knees on the floor.

"What the heck?" Rolling over to a sitting position, Brian gaped at Wiley. "Did we hit something?"

Wiley had cut the motor. The boat slowly settled its wild rocking. "We must have, but I didn't see anything! Are you okay?"

"I think so." Brian sat for a minute, then when the boat was fairly steady he got up and made his way toward the bow. Leaning on his stomach over the front, he checked for damage. Libby crunched herself into the corner to make room for Brian's long, sprawling legs.

Slipping out past Cameron, Wiley squeezed in between Brian and Libby. Laying down next to his friend, he asked, "See anything?"

"Nothing."

Lifting his head, Wiley clapped Brian on the back. "Are you sure you're okay?"

Brian twisted around and sat up. "I'm fine, but check this out!" Blood trickled in thin rivulets from the torn skin of his palms and knees.

"Ugly. It'll hurt like heck in the water. You need some bandages." Standing up to grab the first-aid kit, Wiley called over his shoulder, "What do you think we hit? And *please* tell me again there's no damage!"

"Everything looked okay to me." Brian replied, but he was distracted.

When Wiley returned with the kit, Brian was dabbing his cuts with a tissue mysteriously provided by Libby. He gave the plastic box to her.

"Should I get in and check it out?" Wiley asked, dubiously.

"It's probably a good idea," Brian said. "We got whacked pretty hard. Better you than me."

"Okay, change places."

Brian stood, making space for Wiley to step up ono the seat. The sun's rays penetrated the green-tinged liquid all the way to the bottom. Wiley figured the depth at five or six feet. He pulled off his T-shirt and threw it to Cameron. Then…he just stood there.

"Wiley?" Libby said softly, when he made no move to jump in. Getting no response, she called to him again.

"Look at his chest," Cameron said locking eyes with Libby, when Wiley remained mute. She was sitting by the controls with her eyes glued on him. "He's breathing really hard. What's happening?"

"Wiley," Brian yelled, "snap out of it!"

The teen was openly panting. Sweat poured off his face. Climbing onto the seat to jump in the water had triggered Wiley's most terrifying memory. His father had tossed off his clothes in exactly the same way last May before diving into Lake Erie to rescue a co-worker. Jim Sterling had been snatched off the back of the Grosse Ile police boat by a zombie and pulled down into a watery grave. Watching his dad go after him and disappear into the creature's lair had completely unnerved Wiley. Today's situation had him reliving that moment. He was frozen in terror.

"Wiley, can you hear me?" Brian shouted again.

"I hear you." His voice came out flat, almost robotic.

"Here," Brian said, taking his friend's arm. "Turn around and sit."

"Brian," Cameron whispered, leaving her seat and coming to stand in front of the two boys. "Let's get out of here."

The second blow hit them harder than the first. The front of the craft lifted at least a foot out of the water. Knocked off his feet, Wiley smashed into Brian and then fell past him off the side. He belly-flopped on top of the water with a sickening smack.

"Watch out!" Brian yelled a worthless warning.

Cameron and Libby screamed.

A long, white streak buzzed up from under the boat and swam right at Wiley who was floating face down in the water. The creature dove under the boy and vanished. Wiley's body bobbed crazily.

"Wiley, Wiley!" Brian called in panic. Terrified his friend had already drifted out of reach, Brian bent over the side as far as he could without falling in and stretched out his arm. It wasn't enough. He couldn't reach Wiley.

Dropping to the floor, Libby wrapped her arms around Brian's legs. "Now try!" she yelled.

The side of the boat dug deeply into Brian's pelvis as he leaned forward. Thanks to Libby he gained about four inches, allowing him to hook his finger into the waistband of Wiley's bathing suit. He pulled steadily until his unresponsive friend's body bumped into the boat.

Wiley threw his head up out of the water.

"Wiley?" Brian yelled in his face.

Wiley coughed several times. "I'm okay."

Cameron started to cry.

"Raise your arms and brace your feet against the side," Brian instructed. "I'll pull you aboard."

Wiley followed the instructions and tumbled awkwardly into the craft. He stretched out limply on the floor. The three others huddled around him.

"Are you all right?" Cameron asked through her tears. Wiley had been in the water for less than a minute, but it had felt forever.

Wiley nodded and smiled weakly. "I'm fine."

"Is he really?" Cameron's voice wobbled, as she shifted her tear-filled eyes to Brian.

"Look!" Libby screamed. She was pointing starboard.

Cameron and Brian followed her finger in time to see the white, streaky thing swimming straight at the boat!

"Everyone, get down!" Brian commanded. He and the girls sat immediately, grabbing Wiley and each other tightly. The expected blow never came.

"What is it?" Cameron wailed, as the boat tossed gently. She was hanging onto Wiley's arm with a deathlike grip.

"Maybe an Asian carp?" Libby offered. "They're huge and jump into boats."

"I don't think so," Wiley muttered, struggling to sit up. Cameron's tight grasp on his arm was not helping. "Those suckers can grow to three feet and weigh up to 120 pounds, but whatever came at us was twice that big."

Then, as though to showoff, the enemy sprang out of the water, arched up high in the air and dove back under.

"It's after us!" Cameron shrieked, her face a pasty color. She turned to Wiley, who'd just managed to unclasp her vicious grip. "Did you see it? It's missing a foot!"

"I saw it," Brian cried. "It's hideous!"

Free of Cameron's fearsome hold, Wiley slid along the floor toward the controls. Grabbing the steering wheel, he pulled himself up onto the seat.

The key was still in the ignition. The motor sputtered, then coughed to life. "Cameron," he said, putting out his hand, "come sit with me if you want. Brian and Libby, maybe you should stay on the floor right near us." Wiley waited to see if Cameron would join him. She did. "Okay, here we go."

"The sooner the better!" Brian snuggled closer to Libby as soon as the boat started to move. "Did you see the color of that thing?" he whispered. His lips were almost touching her hair.

"It looked like a ghost." She turned her face towards his, wanting to feel his warm, safe lips on hers.

The third hit nearly capsized them.

It came from the left, and lifted the Whaler so high in the air the right side sunk below the waterline.

"Stay down!" Wiley yelled as water sloshed madly into the boat.

Brian and Libby knocked violently together, struggled to untangle themselves. Cameron had fallen off her perch nearly on top of them. Instinctively all three shifted their weight to the left to counterbalance the boat's tilt. The sunken edge popped back up, cutting off the flow of lake water streaming over the side.

Wiley half-crawled to the front and retrieved three plastic pails from under the seat. "Here!" he yelled to Brian, and threw them. The boat, filled with at least eight inches of water, sat dangerously low.

Leaving them to bail, Wiley returned to the controls. With fingers crossed he turned the key. It took three tries to start the stalled motor. "Hang on," he yelled. Shoving the throttle forward, the clumsy, water-filled craft responded slowly. Reaching into the cubbyhole in front of him, Wiley felt around until his hand touched a waterproof pouch. Grabbing it, he ripped it open with his teeth and extracted his phone.

"Wiley? Is everything all right?"

"No!" he shouted, not caring how wild he sounded. "We're on the other side of Sugar in the same place as Saturday. Something's attacked the boat!"

"You're out on the water?" Jack asked, momentarily confused. He couldn't remember having discussed it.

"Yes, and this *thing* smacked the boat three different times. It almost capsized us! We all saw it!"

"Who's we? Cameron, Libby, Brian and you?"

"Yes."

"Tell me the situation."

"We're okay. I got the boat started and we're headed home."

"Do you know what it was that hit you?"

"It wasn't a fish, that's for sure." Wiley didn't dare name it while they were still out on the water—at its mercy.

"Steve and I are leaving the station with Sander. We'll meet you on the dock."

"Thanks. We're just coming around Sugar."

"Keep it wide open, and don't lose contact with me."

"Will do, but we can't go very fast. The boat's full of water. Everyone's bailing."

"Tell me," Jack said sternly, needing to know the truth. "Do you think it was the zombie?"

"Yes. We saw it."

"Is anyone hurt?"

"Not badly."

Wiley's voice caught slightly, and in that, Jack heard everything he needed to know.

"Stay calm, son. You're doing this exactly right. I'll be with you soon."

27

A LUNCH MEETING

Jack rounded up Steve and Sander. Within minutes of receiving Wiley's call for help, they were in Steve's car with the siren blaring.

"Should we put out an alarm?" Steve asked.

"Probably, but I'd prefer to hear the kids describe what happened in their own words first," Jack explained, wanting to avoid being the cause of hysteria if this turned out to be a false alarm. "Can't you go faster?"

"We mustn't take this lightly," Sander said from the back. "I trust Wiley's judgment, but you are right to proceed with caution, Jack. If you decide this is a real attack it raises so many questions."

At the house Steve squealed to a stop, removed his keys from the ignition, and the three men took off running. From the dock they could see the kids, who hadn't made much progress.

"Should we go escort them in case the thing's still after them?" Jack asked.

"By the time you get the boat going, they'll be back," Steve said.

Jack started pacing.

"It's been awhile since we three were last here," Sander commented drily. More winded than the detectives, he struggled to slow his breathing. Being back together, in this spot, was beyond awkward.

Steve still believed Sander Firth had gone completely crazy last May.

When he, Wiley, and Sander had brought Jack home from the hospital, they had found two trespassers sitting on the Davis dock. It turned out Sander knew one of them. Heidi Beyer had brought her daughter, Sylvia Baron, with her to try and get the two rogue zombies to return. Loose in the world, the creatures were a menace that needed to be stopped. The zombies did as instructed. When they tried to come out of the water onto the Davis dock, Sander shot them.

Steve agreed this was a good thing.

Then Sander had shot Heidi Beyer *and* her daughter, Sylvia Baron. To this day, Sander insisted he'd had no choice. As a Keeper of the Watch he was duty bound to eliminate anyone associated with the darkest of the dark arts.

Steve didn't care how many times the Watcher explained the how and the why, he wasn't buying what the man was selling.

It was a long, convoluted story. Sander had not hesitated to fire on Heidi Beyer after she'd confessed she really *did know* how to bring the dead back to life. And worse still she'd given away the secret to another.

Steve thought what Heidi had done was despicable, even with good reason and she had a good reason. A part of him agreed with Sander nothing but death could stop her from telling others what she knew. Yet, the killing of Heidi in cold-blood without any kind of a trial just felt wrong.

What was even more troubling to Steve was Sander's shooting of his daughter, Sylvia. There was no proof she wasn't completely innocent! The events had happened so fast. Heidi had told Sander Sylvia was his daughter, conceived after a chance meeting and a one-night stand. Sander, completely blindsided by Heidi's announcements, shot both women anyway.

Then he ran.

Steve and Wiley pulled the women out of the river. Heidi was dead. Sylvia was not. Her wound, unlike her mother's, did not end her life.

Steve was grateful, but in retrospect, found it hard to believe a Keeper of the Watch had missed killing someone from such close range. Ever since that day Steve had been suspicious Sander had changed his spots for his daughter, and not followed Keeper of the Watch protocol. In taking the shot he made it look like he was complying, but saved his daughter's life by only wounding her.

"Today the zombie," Sander said, his voice soft and low, "came after the kids. I can't warp my mind around it. Were they a random target? Did it know what it was doing?"

"Wiley only described what it looked like," Jack said, taking Sander's lament literally. "He would know, having seen one before."

"Ah, Wiley," Sander whispered wistfully, closing his eyes for a moment. In the last twenty-four hours this man's world had flipped completely upside down. He knew in his heart Sylvia's abduction so close to the reappearance of the zombie was no coincidence. When he opened his eyes again, he rigorously searched the horizon. "What a bright spot the boy is in this sea of darkness."

After that, they waited in silence. The Whaler barely appeared to be moving.

"I must tell you," Sander finally said in an effort to ease some of the tension, "it is painful enough having to stand on this dock again with you two. I can't imagine doing it with Sylvia. Please, may she be all right." Something like a sob escaped him. He was clearly suffering, and holding in his feelings could not be easy after what he'd been through in the last twenty-four hours. "We were having such a good time yesterday. But the nightmare has begun again. It always does."

When Wiley's ridiculously overloaded boat got close enough for the men to really see, their worry spiked. It looked like a bathtub. Even at full power the boat was cumbersome, and as it neared the dock it was difficult to stop. The teens nearly plowed into the dock. Sander offered a hand each to Cameron and Libby who scampered off the vessel as though it was on fire.

"Any more signs of your attacker?" Jack asked immediately.

"No," Wiley answered.

"Good. Don't worry about the stuff." Jack stepped aboard into water up to his ankles. "Go on up to the house and get dry. We'll finish here and be right with you."

"I'll go with the kids," Sander said, anxious to remove himself from the painful place.

"Sure. David's in the house. Not sure about Linn and Bridget," Jack said. "They went shopping," Wiley called back, already halfway up the yard. "I know. Linn texted me." Jack gave a weary smile. The morning seemed so long ago.

"How odd is it the zombie bombarded this particular boat?" Steve asked the minute they were alone.

Bouncing questions off each other was a professional habit they used to hear each other's thinking and flush out details that might help them solve a case. They'd been doing it since they were rookies.

"Odd? It's freaking bizarre!" Jack replied. "Like everything else these days."

"It made three separate hits on a boat connected to you, and then disappeared without finishing it off and sinking them."

"Sink a Whaler?" For a second Jack fondly remembered Wiley's sales pitch when he'd wanted to buy it so badly. Then he got back to the facts. "The creature didn't do what it's famous for doing: Relentlessly pursuing its target."

"Exactly. It teased them. Zombies don't think. They can't reconsider what they are doing and why. They just dumbly forge ahead. Why did the creature's behavior change today?"

"It's a great question and I have no idea." Jack shrugged. He felt jittery. "We need to find Sylvia. Why it would come after the kids makes absolutely no sense to me."

In the kitchen, Linn and Bridget were putting food on the table. The sight of it made Jack slightly sick, but lunch would probably make him feel better. Missing meals when he was under extreme stress made him mean and sloppy. But neither man stopped on their way to the living room.

"It's after twelve," Jack told everyone. "There's food in the kitchen if anyone wants to get something to eat before we start."

When no one moved, the detectives sat down. Linn and Bridget quietly joined them. The boys couldn't be talked out of their belief they'd encountered the zombie. The girls were less sure.

"Think body parts," Steve prompted. "Did any of you see a face, a leg, or an arm?"

"Yes, but it's kind of a blur," Brian said.

"It's missing a foot. There's just ragged bone," Cameron added, with a shudder.

"Really?" Jack asked in surprise. "It must have been awful to see, but that's a great detail," he told Cameron with a smile.

"A recent wound I wonder? In the last few days," Sander interrupted, "there's been a bit of chatter about a human-like creature seen swimming in the middle of Lake Erie."

Jack's face paled. "I'd not heard."

"My first impression was it was a hoax," Sander continued. "I intended to tell you and Steve today. The night of your party wasn't the right place, then other things got in the way. Now we know the fate of the missing zombie. What intrigues me is why it came after you kids. For this particular creature I would think you, Jack, are its enemy. You fought it. And why attack on the water and not here at the house? Were the kids really its target? How would it know where to find them? Or was it orchestrated on purpose so we'd believe it was nothing more than coincidence?"

"It can't be a fluke," Steve said.

"I agree." Sander looked around the room.

"Sander, tell us more about your thinking," David prompted softly, his voice filled with curiosity.

"Maybe attacking Wiley was a way to get at you, Jack. But that move would be much more sophisticated than anything I believe this creature is capable of executing. It struck three times, then swam away. Something fundamental in how it is operating has changed. Is this creature acting on its own? Or is someone controlling it? If the second is true, what would that mean knowing Frieda and Ernst Karlsson, the creators, are dead?"

Jack felt the room closing in on him. Linn had been right. He'd not believed this could happen. He was the one who had given the kids permission to go out on the water Saturday and they'd all gone skiing yesterday. Suddenly, he looked directly at Wiley. "I don't remember you checking in with me about going out this morning."

Wiley squirmed in his seat. He felt Brian, Cameron, and Libby stiffen. His father's question took the teens by surprise. They'd assumed Wiley invitation this morning was based on parental permission.

"I'm sorry," the boy said directly to his father, but he meant it for everyone. "Today was our last day of summer vacation. You were working, Linn and Bridget were going shopping, and it was another fabulous day to be outside. It just came together."

Jack's eyes drilled into his son. A shadow of the old, cold, Jack Davis momentarily darkened the mood in the room. Then he gave a slight nod of his head and the matter was over. To Jack's credit, he never brought the subject up again.

"What about some lunch?" Linn suggested, unsettled by the rising tension. "Bridget and I have filled the table with goodies. It will give us energy for whatever is coming next."

Steve got to his feet. "Thanks, you two," he said to the women. "I could use some fuel."

"Would you please excuse me," Sander said, rising unsteadily. "I am losing steam. I wonder if I might take a quick shower. I missed one this morning. After that, some food will help immensely."

"Of course," Jack said, graciously. In order to check Sander out of the hospital it had been agreed the Watcher would stay at Jack's at least for the night so he would not be alone. "Come with me and I'll show you your room and get you a towel."

When Sander rejoined them in the kitchen he still looked tired, but far better than he had just minutes ago.

"What can we get you?" Steve offered, vacating his chair.

"Some water to take my pills for my war wounds. Then, as much as I would love a martini, because of the medication I'd best stick with a cup of tea."

Steve smiled warmly. "Coming right up."

Sander settled in Steve's chair. Sighing deeply, he surveyed the assembled group. When a glass of water was put before him he quickly swallowed several pills. "Is there any news of Sylvia?" he finally asked. "Ah, thanks, Steve. Something warm will help!" His swollen and red hands shook as he grasped the cup, but after a few sips his body calmed and he visibly relaxed. As each person filled him in, he listen carefully without interrupting, allowing everyone to have a say.

While Sander had been upstairs, Jack had fanned out the composites drawn from Sander's description of the abductors on the table. Bridget was holding one in each hand and examining them closely.

"Aren't these the guys who live across the canal from you?" she asked Linn. "I think I waved to this one. And he snubbed me."

Sander sat up straight. "Are you sure? That's the con artist who flagged us down."

"Yes," Linn nodded, "I'd say these are the neighbors."

Jack pulled out his phone. His grin couldn't have been bigger. "Thank you one and all! This should get us a warrant to search the Thorofare property." Turning away from them, he moved to the far end of the kitchen to talk without interruption.

"I let down my guard," Sander said quietly to the rest of them. "When we saw this man," he pointed to one of the sketches, "I warned Sylvia not to be too friendly. She accused me of seeing evil in almost everyone and everything around me, so I backed off. I also asked her not get out of the car, but she did anyway. The second her feet touched the ground she was grabbed." Sander looked down at his cup. "I didn't see it happen. I had my eyes closed, sulking because she'd not listened to my advice. This one," he said lifting his head and pointing to the picture of the second man, "snuck around the back of the car. I caught a glimpse of him in the side mirror, but before I could push the lock button he opened the door and pulled me from the seat. How I got to the Sanctuary is a mystery. That is where you boys found me?"

Wiley and Brian nodded.

"Thank you again," Sander said, and lifted his cup in their direction. Then he said what they were all thinking. "Sylvia was taken because these cretins think she knows the Beyer secret."

"Does she?" Jack asked bluntly, rejoining the group. The directness of his question instantly put everyone on high alert again.

"I honestly don't think so," Sander replied with a tired smile. He took the time to meet the eyes of each person at the table. "I've watched and listened carefully over the last months. She went before my colleagues and gained their trust and backing, and they put her through misery. But as you know," and now he frowned, "I've been fooled before."

In many ways the man was a shell of his former self. Beyond the disfiguring physical abrasions, he looked like a tortured soul. His abduction, his missing daughter, and the uncertainty of what was to come, had diminished the proud and invincible demeanor he wore so well.

After finishing his tea, Sander polished off a decent meal. No sooner had he put down his fork, than a halo of light, the color of spun-gold, seeped from his body and encircled them all in a deeply, affirming way.

"We need to gather our power." Sander held them spellbound in his strange, scary, and mystical way. "Agony and suffering come hand in hand with tragedy. It's easy to give in, to lose confidence and momentum. Cataclysmic experiences drain us mentally and physically, rendering us helpless in our fight.

"I can't afford to have it happen to me. I need your help to stay strong to find my daughter. By working together, I can rise above despair. In the past I've mostly gone it alone, but this is way beyond me. I cannot tackle it by myself."

Once again, Wiley found himself inexplicably drawn to this man. The boy drank in every word he said, without any understanding of why. Sander Firth was as human as he, and possessed no gifts or talents that qualified him for superhero status. Yet, he owned a certain power that set him apart from the average person. Wiley was impressed to hear him ask for help. He knew from experience it was not an easy thing to do, and to his knowledge, adults found it nearly impossible.

"Your warm companionship and caring will give me the strength to banish the dark," Sander said, now with something of a twinkle in his eye. "I know as we focus our energies, a positive plan will emerge which will lead us to Sylvia."

They were all a witness to it, and would talk of it for years to come. Right before their very eyes, the terrified father disappeared and a younger, stronger Watcher stood ready for battle.

• • •

"Sander's like a chameleon." Steve was rinsing dishes and loading the dishwasher. He and Jack had offered to do a quick cleanup while the others settled in the living room.

"Ha," Jack laughed. "That's it exactly. At lunch he went from old and frail to young and powerful."

"When you introduced him to the squad room last spring to explain the nature of zombies, he seemed invincible."

"I've been mesmerized ever since I met him in Kroger," Jack admitted. He dunked a sponge under the faucet and wiped the counter. "When I asked him to join us on the raid to the lab at the Karlssons', he said it wasn't his game. He knows his limitations. I sure don't look at myself in that way."

"We each have our own role, and he appreciates that in us. He arms us with his knowledge and something else…."

"Did I ever tell you," Jack broke in, "about the weird dreams I had in the hospital?"

"You can remember?" Steve was so surprised. "You laid there without moving a muscle for days!"

"I couldn't move. I was imprisoned in a heavy blanket of fog. It was urgent I get free. I wasn't safe. I had to get away, but my body was so heavy and I was exhausted."

Steve waited when Jack quit talking. "Go on," he finally urged. He hated hearing the pain in his friend's voice, but whatever Jack was trying to tell him was too important to let it go unheard.

"What I feared most wasn't my injuries," Jack muttered. He shook his head, afraid Steve wouldn't understand. "Zonked out on painkillers, I could feel myself slowly slipping into a drug induced wasteland. If something didn't change soon, nothing of me would be left. I'd become one of them! A zombie! I clung to Sander's words of wisdom to me at our first meeting in Kroger. 'Descent into evil takes time.'"

Steve stopped his cleaning to give Jack his full attention.

"If I didn't fight back they'd take everything from me that makes me human, trapping me forever. I fought as hard as I could to keep them out of my mind, but the color kept fading and the edges of what I could see shrank and turned black."

"What changed?" Steve asked.

Jack gave a funny look.

"Right when I thought I couldn't hold out any longer, I felt this lift. A new picture formed in my mind. I could see I had fallen hundreds of feet down into a very dark, deep crevasse. If I was to survive I had to scale the steep walls back up to ground level. It was a 'how badly to you want it' test. The biggest of my life. I agreed to try." Jack closed his eyes briefly. "The second I said yes everything brightened.

"Seeing Sander do his personal energy thing," he continued, turning to look at Steve, "with Sylvia in the boathouse and healing himself just now at the table, makes me wonder if he had anything to do with my experience? Did he plant that picture of the crevasse in my mind to get me out of that prison?"

"Possibly. He came to see you, more than once."

"Do you know what he did, what he said?" Jack asked.

"No, he always went in alone. You could ask him."

"Hmmm," Jack muttered. "I will, but this isn't the right time. I'm glad he's gained his strength back. He needs to focus on that without distraction. I was afraid Sylvia's disappearance might be too much and destroy him."

"He's pretty tough."

"Yes, but he's taken several big hits lately. He suddenly found, then lost, and then regained a family where once he'd had none. Now his daughter, for whom he has fought desperately, is missing and probably in grave danger."

Steve put the last dish in the dishwasher. "Sander's old patterns of thinking are shifting. He used to view humanity so narrowly. Finding Sylvia has given him permission to be more open to understanding and appreciating the complexities of what it is to be human."

"How weird is it," Jack said, "all three of us are in the same boat, entering into new relationships?" With a smirk, he added, "I wonder what it will do to us."

"It will do good things, Jack," Steve told his friend with great warmth, putting a hand on his shoulder. "Love is a good thing."

• • •

While everyone waited in the living room for Jack and Steve, Wiley turned on the TV. He was flipping channels as the men entered the room.

"Wiley, turn that off, please," Jack said. "We need to concentrate on developing a plan to find Sylvia while we wait for the warrant."

Wiley's finger was on the power button when a Fox News update flashed on the screen.

"The constant barrage of water problems in Detroit and the downriver area," the commentator said, "is multi-faceted and ever changing. Here today are business leaders, Claire Barrett and Eric Beauchamp of Océane Industries."

"Wait!" Linn shouted, pointing at the monitor. "Those two were here, at our party on Friday night! Who are they? Who invited them?"

Framed beautifully on the screen was a stunning couple in their late thirties. The woman, posing subtly for the camera, was physically striking, fastidiously manicured, and dressed in a sharp, stylish outfit guaranteed to make everyone take notice. The man's nonchalant air and impeccable manners created a nice balance to the woman's intensity.

Bridget leaned forward. "I saw them. They were standing several feet away staring at us, remember, Sander? When Steve was introducing me to you and Sylvia."

"Over the past few years," the commentator continued, "their company has lent its expertise to the U.S. to combat and solve some of its most troubling water issues. Ms. Barrett, tell us a little more about why Océane Industries, a foreign based company, is such a good fit to renovate the array of needs being experienced here in Michigan."

"The Great Lakes," the woman began, "are an *international* treasure. Holding so much of the earth's fresh surface water, restoration, protection, and sustainability of its fragile ecosystem is vital. Océane is collaborating with…"

"They were at the party?" Jack interrupted, perplexed. "Why didn't I meet them?"

No one had answers.

"Really? None of us know these two?" Jack threw his hands in the air.

"I do," David said, to everyone's surprise. "They contacted me yesterday with an amazing offer to come work for them at Océane Industries."

"Are you going to accept?" Steve asked, astonished by the news.

"Don't know," David returned with a grin. "I said I'd consider it and get back to them by the end of next week."

"Aren't they just the handsome pair," Bridget said, a bit snidely.

"They were here uninvited on Saturday night," Steve said, thinking out loud. "On Sunday they offered David a job. No one here, besides David, has met them, right?"

Sander smiled slyly. "What a *coincidence*, they're in the water business."

Jack and Steve turned to stare at Sander.

"You know," Sander continued, "I've always suspected there might be others, besides the Karlssons mixed up in this zombie resurrection. We've talked about it."

"Right." Steve said. "The question is, how do we find them?"

"I'm not sure. But see," he told them confidently, "our positive energy is already working. We have a new lead!"

28

A TALK WITH WILEY

MONDAY AFTERNOON, LABOR DAY

"Wiley?" Jack called from the kitchen. He and Linn had drifted from the group in the living room to get some coffee. "Come here a sec."

With a nervous glance at his friends, Wiley got up and left the room. *They've been talking about me,* he thought. *Am I still in trouble for taking out my boat?* Unsure what he was in for, he was relieved when Linn gave him a warm smile.

"Come sit down," Jack said from the table. "Linn and I want to talk through something with you."

After the boy settled in a chair, Jack began. "I haven't been totally forthcoming with you in the last few months. We adults have been trying to protect you."

"From the zombie," Wiley blurted.

"Yes," Jack nodded. "With all the uncertainty about whether it was, or wasn't around, worrying you about it seemed harsh. However, not including you in the conversation was wrong, because you were part of this case from the start. It's rather ironic you've become a zombie target, because our avoiding the topic has kept you uninformed and ill-prepared for an encounter."

Straight talk at last!

"And I've become enlightened." Linn looked mildly amused. "As a doctor, I hate to see any harm come to anyone. All the talk about the missing zombie kept reminding me of how badly it hurt your father. I suggested we keep some of the worst details from you. It may have not been the right thing to do. In fact, I suspect it increased your discomfort. Will you accept my apology?"

"You don't have to apologize," Wiley said, immediately. "I knew why you guys were doing it."

"So you noticed." Jack laughed. "Well, I'm sorry too. We'll try not to do it anymore. If we do, would you let us know?"

"If I can."

"Good," Jack and Linn answered together.

"When the warrant," his father said, getting serious, "comes through we're going to search the house and boathouse. I think that's where we'll find Sylvia. After your adventure this morning, we think her abduction is somehow connected to the zombie. There's no way to know if we'll encounter it, but to avoid talking over the possibility with you doesn't make me look very good. You're part of a very special group that has actually seen one. You know what happened to me the last time. It could happen again."

"Boy, I hope not!" Wiley said with conviction.

"Me, too!" Jack and Linn said together, and they all laughed.

"I know you and your friends told us the details of what happened this morning," his dad continued. "But what about you? Are you okay? It must have been very scary."

"It was." Wiley hesitated.

"What? You can tell us," Jack said.

"I told mom about it," Wiley confessed nervously. "I dream about her a lot, but sometimes I see her. It's happened more than once."

"Wiley, you are so lucky!" Linn clapped her hands with delight. "Tell us more. Not everyone is open enough to receive messages from the other side."

"Messages from the other side?" Bridget echoed, as she floated into the kitchen. "Who's hearing them? I love this stuff!"

Wiley was stunned. "You guys believe me? It's so out there!"

"Hardly." Bridget plunked herself in a chair and flashed him a reassuring grin. "We see it at the hospital, especially in the middle of the night. I suspect many patients get a visit from loved ones who have died, but not all want to talk about it. Those who do describe the experience as much more vivid than a dream. Sometimes they feel a touch or even smell a fragrance. I've walked into a patient's room and enjoyed a whiff."

Wiley grinned with relief and delight. "Both those things have happened to me."

"I've seen her as well," Jack said.

"You have?" his son gasped.

"More than once. Isn't it wonderful to know she's not gone forever?"

"Yes!" Wiley stammered. The subject of his mother had been off limits with his father for so long, it was hard to put everything he was feeling into words. Should he risk saying more? "Knowing she's around," he finally said, "and seeing her happy makes it easier for me. I don't feel like I'm going behind her back by letting new people into my life."

The boy dared to look at Linn. Then, at his father.

"That's it exactly, Wiley." Jack was deeply moved. "It feels like we have her blessing. I couldn't have said it better."

Steve bounded into the kitchen ending their talk. "Sorry to interrupt." He really wasn't, he was pumped for action.

"The warrant?" Jack asked immediately.

"Not yet. Clark's on it. Once again, it's taking longer than usual due to the holiday. However, my gut's telling me we can't waste another moment. I've been on the phone with Clark. He thinks I'm being too proactive, but I want to scout the house again from the road and the canal. Jack, we need to get rocking. There's things we can do."

"Okay. Are we finished here?" Jack asked Linn and Wiley.

They were.

• • •

As Jack and Steve left to organize their departure, Wiley went back to the living room and his friends.

Left together at the table, Bridget turned to Linn. "Everything okay?"

"Yes. Of course I'm worried about what will happen when they go search for Sylvia. But for all the craziness of this weekend, some really good things have come out of it."

"Mm, hmm. Some really good things…," Bridget agreed, with a wink. Her face shone with happiness, but she didn't elaborate.

29

A NEW GAME IN TOWN

MONDAY AFTERNOON, LABOR DAY

Foley and Moreno were at the table on the porch reviewing their plummeting profit margin. Engrossed with their captives in the boathouse, they'd neglected their nefarious business dealings.

"Not good," Foley lamented. Shocked by the low numbers, he realized how spoiled he'd gotten watching the money pile up. When their cash-cow of a zombie had escaped, Foley had tried not to worry it might never reappear and all the money Claire was offering would be lost. He was pretty sure she'd want it, even with it missing a foot.

Moreno agreed with Foley the loss of a big payoff from Océane would be disappointing since they'd already had the sickening thing in their possession, but he'd been relieved when it was gone. He was troubled by something entirely different. "What were the chances those two brats would discover where we dumped Sylvia's father, Mr. Keeper of the Watch?" The news was all over the internet.

Foley looked up. "Yeah, and before he died. Now he can identify us."

"Listen, we've been sloppy and careless and it's gonna get us caught. We'll no longer be the harassers, but the harassees."

"Harassee? Is that a real word?" Foley barked, amused by his partner's distress.

"Who cares? I don't want to go to prison." Moreno countered, glumly.

"Calm down, already. We're figuring it out."

"Well figure this: We've got Sylvia Baron incarcerated. We need to get rid of her!"

Foley closed the account file on the computer and pushed his papers into a pile. "You're right. But things are looking up." He turned in his seat to look at Moreno. "*Syl-v-ia* did everything we wanted, including teaching us how to program the zombie with an iPhone. She's no more use to us, but boy is she good! Can you believe after the thing escaped it came back when we called it? Let me put this stuff away, then we can go to the boathouse. We'll order it to break her neck and drag her body into the lake."

"Can we trust it to really do it?"

"Why not?" Foley blustered, trying not to let his doubt show.

Moreno thought quickly. "Having the zombie kill her makes sense, but not in the boathouse. There's gotta be a better solution."

"Whoa!" Foley exclaimed, as he got out of his seat and looked outside. "Get a load of what's coming down the canal."

It was the enemy!

Gliding serenely past their property, at no more than 5 mph, was the Grosse Ile patrol boat.

"Here we are boys!" Foley taunted softly. "Fooled 'ya didn't we, hiding right here under your nose. Wouldn't it make your day if you knew what we have chained in our boathouse? You better stay ready. A new game in town has started. One I'm calling Catch and Release. It's gonna be great fun. Wanna play?"

As Foley laughed uproariously, Moreno just stared. His crazy partner was almost unrecognizable.

30

THE BOATHOUSE

MONDAY AFTERNOON, LABOR DAY

"What are you thinking?" Jack was driving. They'd just left Hickory and he was at a loss as to where Steve wanted to go.

"Let's start with a drive-by of the Thorofare house." Steve's phone beeped. He read the text to Jack.

> <The patrol boat left the dock on East River and is headed for the canal.>

Jack felt a heaviness settle on him. Intuitively, he'd known for the last few days another showdown of some sort was coming. How could it not? This case was hardly mundane. It involved a zombie! A zombie that had almost killed him.

Unlike the last time they'd had to deal with such evil—when he'd been fully charged to take on anything—he didn't feel ready. Was he scared? Too focused on other things like Wiley and Linn? Complacent? Or worse...did he think he was already good enough at his profession that he didn't have to stay primed? If that was the case, his contribution to the outcome would surely miss the mark of excellence. And considering what they were dealing with, nothing but his best would get him through it safely.

"You're being too hard on yourself," Steve said, when Jack shared his worry. "Depersonalize it, Jack. When have you ever not been ready?"

"Tell me the truth. Was I ready for what we took on in May?"

"You were. We encountered something new, and handled it as best we could. The past is history. We've reviewed it and learned from any mistakes. The future is unknown, it's a mystery that will unravel with time. All we have is now. Focus on it. We'll give whatever we find our all."

"I like what you've said, but we're talking deep-rooted evil. The undead. Hardly the norm. Can anything we do matter?"

"All we do matters," Steve said with conviction.

"It feels out of control to me. Heck, our *normal investigation* these days concerns floating meth labs! When the only real revenue being generated in this stinking economy is from casinos, corrupt corporations, and illegal drugs, what can one little arrest do? Meth labs can spread faster than the Ebola virus. We'll never get rid of it all."

"We'll work to make a dent in whatever we uncover," Steve answered patiently. He was surprised by Jack's feelings, but glad to listen. Jack's rant was piercing an abscess that had grown within him all these months. It had sprouted from doubt and flowered into fear. By letting Jack drain his pain, he might benefit as well. Who knew how much trauma he was harboring? They'd faced something really ugly. "Together, we'll keep our eyes on the prize—a safer downriver area. And guess what, we're not alone, even against something as big as zombies. Look at the team at your house. Remember all we've done to improve the odds. You are totally ready. We're going to keep battling every spot of infection we find."

"What about when we miss some?"

"We will," Steve said easily, "and it will hurt to fail. But we can't be so afraid to make a mistake that it keeps us from doing our job. We'll keep going after them, as always. It's about the trying."

When Jack didn't say anything, Steve shared one last thing. Something of his own. "I'm going to try again, too, in my personal life. Bridget and I are engaged."

Jack immediately stopped brooding and beamed as brightly as the sun. "That's great! When did you decide?"

"Last night. Will you be my best man?"

"Yes! I'd be honored. You've set a date?"

"We're thinking next February. Valentine's Day weekend."

"Nice." Jack took out his phone. "It's on the calendar."

Steve grinned widely as they turned onto Thorofare Road. Then both men became all business.

• • •

Sylvia had done everything her abductors had asked of her in the hope of staying alive. She had to find her father.

After inserting the chip into the zombie's head and it escaped, she'd instructed her captors how to control its behavior and get it back. She'd even added a test run to prove how well the chip worked, that she was legit, and not out to scam them. The call to return was so strong the zombie had obeyed. Satisfied with her work and terrified of the creature, the men had left her alone after forcing her to take two sleeping pills.

Currently, she was huddled, her brain muddled, in a corner of the boathouse with her head hanging nearly in her lap. This last unaccounted lapse of time scared her more than the others.

She was untied, untethered, and untended. Well, untended wasn't quite right. The zombie was back, chained to the wall again by its other ankle. The terribly ravaged eyes stared blankly. Could it see her? She wasn't sure.

The thing showed no concern over the loss of its foot, or to the ugly snake-like things clinging to the hole in its shoulder. Sea lampreys. They were about two feet long. Their circular mouths were clamped down on their food trying to suck out any available bodily fluids. What nourishment they might obtain from the putrefying flesh of a zombie was beyond Sylvia's imagination.

A sound from the canal diverted her attention. Swiveling her head toward the boat slip, the rumble of a motor beyond what looked like a garage door that cut off the building's interior from the water was getting louder. Scrambling to her feet was an effort. In no shape to swim to freedom, she threw open her arms and let loose a heart-stopping scream. She screamed and screamed until she wilted to the floor, dizzy and panting so hard her chest hurt.

"Help me," she tried to scream again. Her voice failed her. Desperate to be free, she ran to the door used by her captors and pounded on the metal. "Help me! I'm locked in here!"

A heavy thump made her jump back from the door.

"Grosse Ile Police. Who's in there? Are you all right?"

"Help!" Her scorched voice cracked like an adolescent boy's. "My name is Sylvia Baron. Help me, please!"

"Sylvia, it's Steve. Jack is with me. The door is dead bolted and it's metal. We're going to try and break it down, but we may need a blowtorch."

"Be careful," she rasped. "The zombie is in here and there are two men somewhere outside."

At the sound of voices the zombie came to life. Sylvia turned in time to see it pull itself off the floor and lean back against the wall.

The noise outside became deafening. Then suddenly it stopped.

"Sylvia, can you hear me?" Steve yelled. "The door won't budge. We've sent for tools. Hang in there, it won't be long."

"Steve, the banging has agitated the creature! I'm going to swim out through the boat slip. I have to get out of here!"

"Sylvia, this is Jack. Is the zombie free?"

"No it's chained to the wall."

"Then give us five minutes more! Your father is on his way here. Stay with us. You don't want to miss him."

"My father's okay?" she cried, delighted and stunned by the news.

"Yes! Please, try and stay calm. He'll be with you soon."

Later, she would not remember much about waiting to be rescued. The blowtorch was loud and the tip of the flame, as it cut through the lock bolt like a knife through butter, got bigger and brighter as she readied herself for her rescuers. Before the door could be opened, there was shouting.

"What the hell are you doing?" It was the driver. "Get away from that door! This is private property."

"Robert Foley? We have a warrant to search the residence and boat-house. If you make one more move to stop us, I will arrest you." Jack commanded with authority.

Sylvia jumped again as the door burst open. Swinging hard on the hinges, it banged the wall behind it, then bounced back.

First through the opening was Steve. Sylvia threw out her hands and he grabbed them. Next came the driver and the second man, ushered in by two officers. Jack and Sander were last.

"Father!" Sylvia cried, her eyes alight with relief, and something much deeper.

He did not come to her.

"Everyone freeze!" Sander stood tall and straight, and slightly aglow, inhabiting the persona of a warrior pumped for battle. Tall and imposing, he ignored his daughter, directing his full attention elsewhere.

Confused and panicked by the snub, Sylvia looked to see what held her father's attention. What could be more important than she?

The malevolent presence! The lame zombie, hideous to observe with its blistered white skin and gray, bloodless lips cracked and ringed with sores, stood teetering on one leg. The black, snake-like tubes swung gently from the hole in its shoulder.

Several guns fired.

The creature, provoked by the commotion, puffed out its chest and ripped the chain from the wall with its hands. It bounded forward, dragging the chain, and hit Foley and Moreno in the face. The blows were so powerful, nose cartilage shoved into their brains killed them instantly.

Next it turned to Sylvia, absorbing bullet after bullet without pause.

"Sylvia, take my energy. Use it!" Sander extended his arms like prongs on an electrical plug. The air sizzled and popped around them.

Sylvia's body began to glow. As though a three-way bulb had been turned from dim to bright, the strength of her energy visibly escalated incrementally. When she reached full power she broke the connection with her father and held out her own arms toward the zombie. Mini balls of fire, no larger than marbles, flew off her fingers smashing into the creature's chest.

The zombie dropped to its knees. Putting its hands on the ground, it scurried back toward its watery exit.

"Look," Jack shouted, pointing to the water. "How?"

A lone head—a new reanimation—was there, bobbing in the water.

The worn-torn zombie dropped noisily into the water with a big and loud splash. Both creatures instantly disappeared.

"How could that slimy thing slip out of our grasp again? And now there's another one?" Jack cried. He ran to the water and fired round after round into the dark depths below.

"Isn't life just full of surprises?" Sander, spent from his energy exchange with Sylvia, sat down wearily. "Never in a million years would I have guessed this outcome."

• • •

The creature was no longer alone. Like the liquid in which it swam, the presence of another added another layer of comfort.

Its ragged body, weighted down by the chain, was disintegrating a piece at a time. First the eyes, then the shoulder, its skin, a foot…sea lampreys.

How long did it have? How long could it keep going?

• • •

31

A HOLIDAY CELEBRATION AT LAST

MONDAY NIGHT, LABOR DAY

The showdown at the boathouse was over. Sylvia was safe and Foley and Moreno were dead.

After a consensus was reached on how to alert the public about this newest zombie development, Jack and Steve left the drudge work of dealing with the remains of the two men, plus the gruesome appendage left behind by the zombie, in the hands of Javier Day. He and officers Hall Kriak and Todd Kelly, plus a few others, had been part of the team that put together clues and eventually raided the scientists' lab last May.

So Jack and Steve were back home on Hickory by 7 p.m. Sylvia, battered from her ordeal but refusing to go to Urgent Care was with them, and Sander was not letting her out of his sight.

Although they passed party after party, and smelled one barbeque after another on their drive back to Hickory, there was little holiday spirit evident in any of them as they came through the kitchen door.

The atmosphere changed quickly after they were welcomed home by Wiley, Linn, Bridget and David. With drinks in hand, everyone congregated around the kitchen table and took turns telling their stories.

David had made guacamole and salsa from ingredients found in the fridge. He'd grated three kinds of cheese and melted it onto flour tortillas which he served hot.

"There's a new one?" Wiley asked in wonder. He'd been shocked to hear the news, but it felt good to bring up the subject and not be rebuffed.

"Yes," Sander nodded to Wiley, "From the little we could see, it looks in good condition." Turning to Sylvia, he said, "With this new development it's more important than ever we have your help. So far, we've focused too much on the details of this invasion. If we are to do any good, we must discover the matrix, the point of origin."

Sylvia's insides quivered. She hadn't explained all she'd done for her captors in order to stay alive. Was now the right time? Should she say it in front of Wiley? Fearing it was really just her pride keeping her from telling the truth, she risked losing their respect and told of her weakness. She'd done everything her abductors had asked to gain her freedom. When she got to the part about programing the zombie to bombard a boat, every face at the table turned white.

Sure that her lack of defiance had disgusted them into silence, she said the obvious. "I seem to have hit a nerve."

Sander explained. "Wiley and his friends were out in his Whaler this morning. A long white thing attacked their boat three times, almost capsizing them."

It was Sylvia's turn to go pale. "It worked? I didn't know. I was showing off to look valuable. What were the chances it would attack the kids?" she whispered.

"Sylvia," Jack said, hoping to redirect her attention, "no worries. You did what you had to do." He wanted to hear exactly what she'd done to the creature, but it felt too gruesome a conversation for the moment. "I've never seen anything like the light show between you and your father. What did that feel like?"

Jack, filled with compassion, watched her face and felt her pain. Although no one seemed to remember—and he wasn't going to tell them—he had just come face to face with the monster that had almost killed him. Fear, hatred and disgust had washed over him at seeing it again. Steve had advised him not to make it personal on the way to the boathouse. But it was, wasn't it? Only now that he felt safe—if only momentarily for it could still find him…still get him—was he able to internalize all he'd survived last May. And worst still, it had gone after Wiley.

Grateful for Jack's rescue, Sylvia said, "I was so exhausted after what I'd been through…then I was filled with such strength! While visiting the Isle of Man, I learned my great-grandmother and grandmother could utilize energy they absorbed. Father says he lacks the skill. I didn't do anything special today. What happened just happened. As energy poured into me, it replenished my stamina and restored my balance. My goal is to learn to channel this gift, if I get the chance. For what purpose, I can't imagine."

The conversation drifted to the mysterious Océane executives and their bold move to crash the party. Because no one could see any purpose behind what they'd done, it aroused suspicion but they found no answers.

Sylvia sat speechless. Claire Barrett had re-entered her life. Should she honor her secret pact with the Océane Exec to never reveal they had met? Or give up valuable information that could help those sitting with her tonight?

"David," Sander said thoughtfully, surprising them all, "I think you should accept Océane's job offer, but work for us undercover. Claire Barrett and Niles Beauchamp need watching."

Sylvia's stomach clenched in a knot.

David laughed, fully amused by the idea of playing spy. He quickly sobered when he found Sander wasn't kidding.

Jack flashed David a wicked grin. "I would personally love it if you would. What an excellent payback for coming here uninvited."

"Could they be the unknowns?" Steve asked suddenly.

"Hmm, I wonder. Let me give it some thought," Sander said. "After a good night's sleep we can break it all apart tomorrow."

"I'll do some background checking," David offered.

"You're on," Sander said.

Sylvia opened her mouth, then quickly closed it.

"Try not to talk," Linn advised, assuming Sylvia's facial wounds were causing her discomfort.

Bridget was already on her feet in search of a paper towel to mop up the liquid oozing through the heavy layer of salve she'd applied to Sylvia's face.

Sylvia smiled weakly in thanks, then closed her eyes. Her distress had nothing to do with her physical injuries. *How could I have escaped being trapped in the boathouse, only to be trapped by what I know?* The party crashers *were* Claire and Niles! They *were* linked to the zombie. They *were* the unknowns!

But if she told what she knew, Claire at least would brand her a whistle-blower. Could she live with breaking her word, even for a good reason?

There must be a way for her to justify sharing her secret. Secrets, secrets, secrets! If this scenario played out, and David did go to work for Océane as an undercover agent, how could she keep working with her father, Jack, and Steve, and now possibly David if she kept quiet?

She needed time to think. If she told the truth would Claire come after her? It would also mean she'd be breaking a promise to her mother. And she'd lied to her father and the Keepers of the Watch. Would they understand her dilemma? How hard it was for her to choose sides? Or would they call her a traitor?

Crushed by weight of this new predicament, on top of everything she'd endured, it was impossible to come to a decision right now. Her face burned, her body hurt, and she was so tired. Sitting back heavily in her chair. Sylvia gave herself twenty-four hours to recover, analyze the situation, and find not just an answer, but the right answer.

Bridget got up to lite the grill, pleased that everyone had found an appetite and enjoyed the hors d'oeuvres. She'd shucked a bunch of corn to roast with some kosher hotdogs. It was a wonderful meal and at the end, David surprised them with dessert.

"Cherry pie?" Jack and Wiley said at the same time. They loved pie!

"Is there ice cream?" Steve asked.

"Vanilla." Bridget burst out laughing. "Didn't I tell you he would ask," she said to Linn.

When no one could eat another bite, Bridget broke the good news. "Steve and I are engaged. The wedding will be next February, Valentine's Day weekend."

Everyone cheered, and all the men, including Wiley, gave Bridget a kiss. Jack opened a bottle of champagne that had been in the fridge since New

Year's. Even Wiley was given a smidgeon. When everyone had a glass, Jack said, "To Bridge and Steve. I am so thankful for your friendship and love. I wish you the very best, now and forever."

"Now and forever!" came the rousing reply.

• • •

Wiley ran upstairs after half-heartedly helping with the dishes. He'd been shooed away so he could get ready for school. In his room, he checked his phone. He was dying to tell Cameron Sylvia was safe, Bridget and Steve's good news, and he'd gotten to taste champagne. He smiled to see she'd texted. But her message filled him with terror.

<Truth. Did you kiss Stevie Gail at the party?>

"Brian, you jerk!" Wiley raged out loud. "You screwed me!" Parker, asleep on the bed, raised his head in alarm when Wiley's phone almost hit him.

It was the hardest call Wiley had ever made.

"Well?" Cameron said, instead of hello. Her voice was cold, demanding.

"Yes. After you left. She asked me to dance and then we got something to drink. She gave me a kiss before she went home." Wiley confessed as fast as he could, using his words carefully to make it sound like it wasn't his fault. It didn't help.

"How could you? We are over! You're scum. First the zombie is after you, then you cheat on me, and lie about it. This kiss was hardly so innocent, from what I hear. Don't ever call or text me again." She cut the connection.

Wiley couldn't breathe. He'd not meant to hurt her.

What. Had. He. Done?

32

THE UNKNOWNS

Yesterday Claire and Niles had presented their offer to the city of Detroit on Fox News. A Labor Day present for a city of laborers! An explosion of phone calls, texts, and meetings had overwhelmed them and eaten up much of their day. The city and the surrounding communities, who depended on Detroit for their potable water, were ecstatic. Océane Industries would provide a sense of security that was currently sorely lacking.

The high praise and collective sigh of relief from a thankful source thrilled Claire. The trip to Michigan had been productive, other good things were in the works. David Stryker had been contacted and he'd agreed to consider their proposal. Niles was optimistic. As he said, how could David turn them down after all they'd offered?

Both she and Niles were unsettled over the death of Foley and Moreno, but for very different reasons. Claire was sure Niles was thrilled taking ownership of the zombie had alluded her. She was furious Foley and Moreno had found the creature and kept it secret, but was captivated by the report a new one had been spotted.

When Frieda and Ernst Karlsson/Roth had originally come to Océane Industries seeking capital for their grand scheme, they'd sworn their offer to create and provide creatures was exclusive. Every time Claire thought about that conversation, she wondered. Had the scientists lied and sold some to others behind Océane's back? Or was someone else in the manufacturing business? Claire longed to know more details. Did the new zombie look the same? Was it acting differently? Responding better?

Because of these questions, Claire couldn't get back to France and Océane's headquarters fast enough. There she'd have privacy to access search engines that could dig deeper and more thoroughly than anything available to her here. No one else needed to know what she was doing. After these last few days with Niles, she felt a touch of sorrow in not being able to share this with him. His continued lack of understanding with her infatuation was so infuriating!

There was some excellent news, though. Sylvia Baron had kept her distance and kept her big, fat mouth shut about what she knew. Plus, their escapade at the party remained unknown. It had been a stupid risk, but think of what they'd learned!

With her mind whirling, Claire stood with Niles on the deck of the Océane II ready to board their helicopter. Looking out at the endless expanse of blue, Claire said, "Water, water, everywhere..."

"Yes. It's beautiful."

"Exquisite." Claire was looking forward to the future in a way that had been lacking for months. The lull in her life was over. There was much to uncover, much to discover. She was ready. Bring it on!

33

SCHOOL'S IN FOR WIN-TAH

TUESDAY MORNING, THE DAY AFTER LABOR DAY

"Stop! Please stop!"

Wiley had been so deeply asleep he didn't hear the buzz of his phone alarm the first time it went off. Forcing himself out of bed, he crossed the room, and grabbed the irritant from the top of his dresser. "Shut up!" This silly routine worked to get him going and not be late for school, but it made him cranky.

Rain was beating on the roof. There was nothing to see but gray out his window. Summer was definitely over, at least for him, although technically the fall equinox was not for several more days.

Wiley eyed his bed longingly, but his father would kill him if he was late. Halfway to the bathroom he remembered. He and Cameron were kaput… over…broken-up…splitsville. *Brian, you traitor! I so hate your guts!* Wiley had figured Brian would stay mad for a while, then get over it, and the two of them would go on as always. Never in a million years had he considered *his best friend* might run to Cameron and *tell on him*!

"Breakfast." His father's voice boomed up the stairway.

"Just getting in the shower, be right down."

Wiley raced through his morning routine. In his room, he threw on whatever he could find, grabbed his backpack and sports bag, and went downstairs. As he entered the kitchen the mouthwatering smells of cinnamon, freshly brewed coffee, and Wiley's favorite—bacon—nearly made him sick. Appreciating that his father had done this especially for him, he managed a few bites. Then he pushed the leftovers around on his plate until he dared to get up and throw the rest away.

Jack Davis was so engrossed in reading about yesterday's raid at the boathouse he didn't look up. The lack of commentary about how his son was dressed, or how he should act at school was a bit of help. For a second, Wiley wondered what the outside world was saying about the zombies, but he didn't dare risk drawing attention to himself by asking. If his dad noticed he wasn't himself and started inquiring if something was wrong, Wiley knew he'd fall apart. Using his father's distraction with the day's news to his advantage, the boy got up, put his plate in the dishwasher, and gathered his things.

The minute he was out of the house, his outrage toward Brian grew with each step he took. It was still raining, but he barely noticed the trickle running down his back until the dark sky rumbled with thunder. He was a sight. His hair was plastered to his head and his clothes were totally soaked. Bringing an umbrella or jacket had never crossed his mind.

By the time he got to the bus stop, he was ready for a showdown. The bus halted right in front of him and Wiley could see Brian through a window. He felt the shock the second he stepped aboard and looked down the center aisle. For the first time in years, the seat next to Brian wasn't empty. His best friend was casually laughing about something with someone else.

Slipping into a vacant seat in the second row, Wiley rode solo for the entire trip in cold, wet misery. After exiting the bus, he hung back and waited for Brian to come down the steps.

"You jerk!" Wiley's white-hot anger exploded the minute they were face to face.

Brian said nothing. Several kids turned to stare, drawn instinctively to the angry tension. The boys moved away, smoldering silently as they waited for the bus to empty and they could be alone. Snippets of music started and stopped around them as the marching band prepped some more for Friday's first football game of the season.

Wiley raised his voice to be heard over the drums, but the intensity of his feelings nearly choked him. "You had to tell her, didn't you?"

"What? It wasn't me," Brian yelled back, his face flushing from being attacked. "I saw you, but I didn't tell Cameron. How can you think I would? She texted me last night and told me who did tell her, and to let me know she was through with you." Brian shrugged, at a loss to understand. Then, he walked away, through with Wiley too.

Wiley remained where he was, blinking in astonishment. It wasn't Brian? Then who had betrayed him? Brian hadn't said and he couldn't ask Cameron.

He walked through the school doors in a trance to find Cameron talking to Colin Woods, a half-back on the football team and a person of interest to her last spring. There was no other way for Wiley to get to his locker, than to go right past them. Sucking in his breath, he plowed forward trying to hide the emotional chaos in which he was drowning. Insane thoughts rushed through his head. If he'd taken Linn and Bridget's offer to go shopping yesterday, he might have on something more interesting than grubby shorts and an okay T-shirt. He'd never gotten the haircut he needed, like the one that looked so good on Brian. Meanwhile Colin, Wiley saw from the corner of his eye, looked pretty great, and so did Cameron.

Wiley kept his head down as heat burned up his neck. What was Cameron saying to Colin? Did the whole school know his life story? Like a punch in the gut, another terrible thought came to him. Surely, as soon as McKnight and his vicious gang heard the gossip, they'd use it against him for all it was worth.

His Cameron misery ended abruptly.

Stevie Gail was leaning back against the wall directly across from his locker.

I guess the whole school does know my business.

Without saying hello he threw his sports bag on the floor and fumbled with his combination. When the lock opened he quickly took off his backpack and started unloading everything he didn't need for the next two periods. Hiding his face in his locker, his mind raced. *How did she know where to find me?* It took him just seconds. Lockers were assigned alphabetically by grade. Her last name started with G, his with a D. Last year her locker would have been right near here in the same hallway.

He turned his head at the smell of her shampoo. She was so close he could feel her body heat.

"I heard you and Cameron are no longer together," she said softly. "Is it because of me? If so, I'm sorry."

Wiley felt nothing but wariness. Warning bells rang in his head. He needed to be very careful here. It might be because of his bad mood, but something felt off. Stevie's smile didn't quite match the tone of her apology. Was this fun for her? Was she toying with him? What could she possibly want? Was there really a chance a sophomore girl would be interested in a freshman boy?

No WAY!

It was never going to happen. Older girls did not date younger boys. Even if he was interested in her, and he wasn't sure that was the case, he couldn't think of a single way he could heighten his profile enough to catch her attention and become acceptable. Crew was not the sport to make a name for yourself. *Maybe Dad was right in thinking football was the way to do high school.* His grades were good, but so what?

Stevie was definitely playing with him, and he wanted no part of it.

The adrenaline rush of frustration and anger that had fueled him for the last hour drained away, and the morning's drama lost its hold on him. He stopped what he was doing and looked her full in the face.

"There's no need to apologize," he said quietly. "Whatever we did, Stevie, I own my part. Thanks for stopping, but I need to keep moving. I don't want to be late on the first day."

Wiley tried to laugh, but it sounded pretty fake. Pushing his locker door closed, he spun the dial.

Stevie nodded and moved to leave. After three steps she turned back. "Are you going to the football game on Friday?"

"Don't know. I haven't thought about it." Wiley swung his backpack over his shoulder.

"I'll look for you." She smiled again. This time it looked more sincere.

Wiley said nothing. Walking in the opposite direction, he kept up a chatter of "hey, how are you?" until he reached the biology lab. He found a seat in the middle of the room and took a pencil and pad from his backpack. By the time the bell rang for the period to start, the room was nearly full. As the teacher began to explain what was expected, Wiley was nearly crushed anew by a terrible vision. This school year, the one he'd wished so hard would be the best ever, was off to a horrendous start. The next nine months stretched endlessly before him. In the last twenty-four hours he'd lost his girlfriend, his best friend, and he was now being teased by a tenth grade flirt.

For a second, he fantasized about going to the office and saying he was sick. He could go home, get in his boat, and escape to Sugar. Even in the rain! But suddenly he found himself holding a cicada. After being given a magnifying glass, an information sheet, and a questionnaire, he was put to work. School was back in session.

● ● ●

Home at last, Wiley dragged himself inside. He closed and locked the door and reset the alarm. Pushing his sports bag with his foot, he inched it toward the basement where the washing machine would transform his pile of smelly clothes back into something manageable.

His father and Linn were at the kitchen table, their heads almost touching. This time when he came into the room, Wiley sensed no tension. Whatever the adults were discussing did not appear to be a secret.

"Wiley!" The pleasure in his father's voice warmed his heart. "You look beat. Come and sit and tell us about your day."

"It seemed to go on forever." He dropped into a chair. The dour look on his face spoke volumes. "And it's not over. I have homework!"

"Dinner is almost ready," Linn told him sympathetically. "Food will help."

Having eaten practically nothing all day, Wiley was surprised to find something smelled good. His stomach growled.

"We're having roast chicken, mashed potatoes, and a salad," Jack told him, knowing these were some of his favorite foods.

"Gravy?" Wiley was suddenly starving.

"Gravy," Jack said. "Hey, I heard today we missed something remarkable over the weekend. A mini-submarine tied up at the Yacht Club. Get this, it had a bubble top made of some kind of plastic. When you're sitting in it you can see all around you. Imagine cruising around the lake in such a thing!"

"We missed it?" Wiley replied, crestfallen. "I've seen pictures of mini-subs online and I want one!" Before he knew it, he was sharing his dreams of how he'd use one if given the chance. "I've been checking out Northwestern Michigan College in Traverse City. The Great Lakes Water Studies Institute is a part of it and they have a hands-on, freshwater studies curriculum. Using some amazing research vessels, you get to apply what you learn to real life issues. You leave there with an associate's degree after two years and you can streamline elsewhere to get a bachelor's degree."

"If you're serious," Linn said, "why don't we take a road trip up north and check out the campus? I'm happy to call and make an appointment so you can ask questions and get a tour."

"REALLY?" Wiley's grin was huge, his grueling day forgotten. "You would do that for me?" He was thunderstruck. He was so used to being lectured to by adults and not heard. Parents, teachers, know-it-alls were always trying to shove their ideas onto kids, without allowing them to say much of anything in return. That had been one of the things so great about Cameron. They had talked. She had listened.

"Absolutely!" Linn laughed. "I would really enjoy it. What do you say, Jack?"

"I'm in! What if we wait until crew season is finished? Then we can drive up on a Thursday after school and visit the campus on Friday. That will give us Saturday to just fool around."

Thoroughly psyched, Wiley opened his mouth to ask if Brian could come too. Then he remembered. Brian wasn't talking to him anymore. But in the warm kitchen, with Linn and his dad, loneliness couldn't touch him. He felt okay for the first time all day.

• • •

After dinner, Wiley went to his room to do his homework. His phone didn't beep or ring once. Parker, as always, kept him company. When the teen finally crawled into bed, he was too tired to read. Instead, he spend a few minutes thinking about Cameron and Stevie. Had he really told Stevie he 'owned whatever was between them?' All in all, he decided smiling slightly to himself, it was a pretty good line. He still didn't understand why he'd done what he did with her, but there was no taking it back.

Most of today had been spent in a haze. He couldn't imagine anything about what lay in store for him next week, or next month. To stop worry from creeping in and taking hold, he snuggled down in the covers. He was home. He was safe. Anguish had ruled his day. Past circumstances and the emotions evoked had blown his stability—until he'd gotten home. If he could hold on for a little bit longer, he'd be all right.

Eventually, he allowed himself to close his eyes. He listened to Parker's slow breathing. With no warning, he felt his mother's light touch on his forehead. For the second time that night, Wiley's loneliness and worry evaporated. Soon, he was asleep.

• • •

The current tugged at its legs. Sand shifted beneath its feet. The cool, loving liquid rippled softly around its neck. From time to time, like a submarine's telescope, it poked its head above the water to keep a lookout.

To stand and watch.

There were more people, more boats. More commotion. What did this mean? It didn't know. It couldn't understand. Settling in the silt, a nest of sorts, it rested with the other.

And waited for instructions.

• • •

EPILOGUE

Parker's running leap off Wiley's bed woke him. He panicked, seeing the clock. Was he late? No, today was Thanksgiving. There was no school.

Snuggling under the covers, Wiley listened to the music and laughter coming from downstairs. Maybe Linn was back from doing rounds at the hospital. Bridget was working until 3 p.m., and then would join them. Last night, Steve and his father had hooked up an extra flat screen TV. Jack Davis would be in his glory today, and thankful for game after game of football. With 3 screens available to him, he wouldn't miss a one.

Also coming for the day were Sander and Sylvia, David Stryker and his girlfriend, Freddi Hackett. No other kids would be there, but Wiley still thought the day would be okay.

He gave a minute's thought to Brian and Cameron. He knew both were out of town, even though neither were talking to him.

Eventually, when he could no longer ignore the mouth-watering smell of roasting turkey or his growling stomach, he put his feet on the floor and started his day.

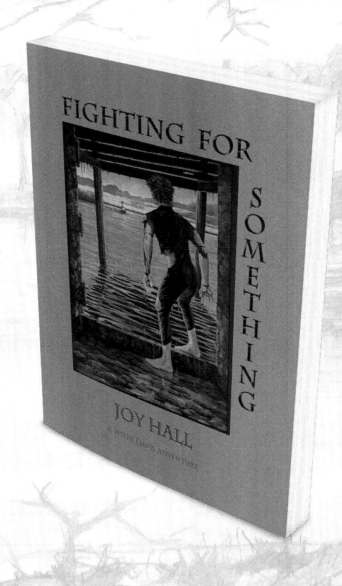

31240409R00126

Made in the USA
Middletown, DE
23 April 2016